92.

CU00894959

'I don't want your money, Mr Jarrett.'

He shrugged. 'Whatever you say.' He sounded weary of the whole situation. 'Well, let me know if I can be of assistance to you in any way.'

'Are you married?'

'Heaven forbid!' he burst out. 'I trust you're not suggesting that I should step into my cousin's shoes as your fiancé?'

Nicola said smoothly, 'That *is* what I was going to suggest.'

Dear Reader

Here we are once again at the end of the year...looking forward to Christmas and to the delightful surprises the new year holds. During the festivities, though, make sure you let Mills & Boon help you to enjoy a few precious hours of escape. For, with our latest selection of books, you can meet the men of your dreams and travel to far-away places—without leaving the comfort of your own fireside!

Till next month,

The Editor

Marjorie Lewty was born in Cheshire, and grew up between there and the Isle of Man. She moved to Liverpool and married there. Now widowed, she has a son, who is an artist, and a married daughter. She has always been drawn to writing and started with magazine short stories, then serials and finally book-length romances which are the most satisfying of all. Her hobbies include knitting, music and lying in the garden thinking of plots!

STEP IN
THE DARK

BY

MARJORIE LEWTY

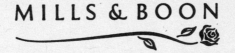

MILLS & BOON

MILLS & BOON LIMITED
ETON HOUSE, 18-24 PARADISE ROAD
RICHMOND, SURREY TW9 1SR

All the characters in this book have no existence outside the imagination of the Author, and have no relation whatsoever to anyone bearing the same name or names. They are not even distantly inspired by any individual known or unknown to the Author, and all the incidents are pure invention.

All Rights Reserved. The text of this publication or any part thereof may not be reproduced or transmitted in any form or by any means, electronic or mechanical, including photocopying, recording, storage in an information retrieval system, or otherwise, without the written permission of the publisher.

MILLS & BOON and the Rose Device
are trademarks of the publisher.

First published in Great Britain 1994
by Mills & Boon Limited

© Marjorie Lewty 1994

Australian copyright 1994

ISBN 0 263 14114 4

Set in Times Roman 10 on 11½ pt.
07-9410-55520 C

Made and printed in Great Britain

CHAPTER ONE

THERE was a swish of brakes and the train began to slow down.

In a corner seat of a nearly empty second-class carriage Nicola Oldfield consulted the list of stations she had scribbled down as a guide before leaving Charing Cross. She wasn't familiar with this part of West Kent—well, she wouldn't be, would she? This was millionaire-land and not her usual line of country. Yes, the next stop was Dunton Green, where Paul would be meeting her. She uncrossed her long, slim legs, smoothed down her already satin-smooth light brown hair, picked up her white plastic handbag and the lacy shawl Gran had insisted on her bringing in case the June evening turned chilly, and sat forward expectantly, looking out of the window.

'We're rather out in the country,' Paul had said when he'd phoned her this morning to invite her to his mother's Saturday night party. 'But I'll meet you at Dunton Green. Don't be late.'

He'd hung up rather abruptly and Nicola had grinned to herself. In the six months she'd worked as his secretary she'd watched Paul Jarrett's technique with a succession of girlfriends. When he began to hang up abruptly on them it meant that he was on the verge of ditching them. She wasn't his girlfriend, although after the extraordinary events of last evening she might be forgiven for believing that she was next on the list.

She and Paul had been working late, to prepare for his trip to France next week, and afterwards he had taken her out for a meal at a small restaurant near the office. She'd noticed that he'd had a good deal more to drink than usual and when they'd got into the taxi that would take her to her station he had become distinctly amorous and had tried to persuade her to come back to his flat 'for a coffee'. Knowing Paul, she'd known what this would mean but was surprised, because he'd never made a pass at her before. She'd decided to treat it as a joke and had told him that she didn't approve of a secretary having an affair with her boss.

'Affair?' he'd muttered thickly into her neck, while his hand had groped for the buttons of her blouse. 'Who said anything 'bout an affair? I want us to get married, Nicky, darling. Wanted you for ages. C'mon, sweetheart, we'll have a good time.'

'Don't be silly, Paul. You've wanted a lot of other girls.'

'No,' he'd insisted. 'No, only you, darling; you're the—the one and only.'

She'd managed to hold him off until the taxi arrived at the station. Paul's last words had reached her through the open window. 'Don't f'get, my lovely. Ask you again Monday morning.'

Nicola had smiled to herself as she'd walked away. By Monday morning he'd have only a hazy recollection of what he'd said. She might even tease him a little about it. She'd giggled to herself all the way home, thinking of his face.

But when she'd reached the semi-detached house in Watford where she lived with her grandmother, the amusement had disappeared abruptly. She'd found Gran in a terrible state. She'd just heard on the local news that there had been a nasty attack on a girl who lived in the next road and the police had issued a warning that the man might strike again.

Gran had been trembling with nerves. 'Of course I shan't go away next week and leave you alone,' she'd quavered. 'I wouldn't dream of it.'

Nicola had thought quickly. 'But Gran, dearest, you must go,' she'd said firmly. 'And you won't be leaving me on my own. Paul Jarrett, my boss, has just asked me to marry him. I'm engaged, Gran. Isn't that lovely? And of course Paul will look after me while you're away. He'll probably take me to stay with his mother.'

There had been a great deal of talking after that. Gran had been amazed, as well she might be, Nicola had thought wryly. She had never mentioned Paul Jarrett except sometimes in connection with her work, and the old lady had not known whether to be thrilled about the engagement or worried about dangerous news. 'I'll have to meet your young man,' she said finally, when Nicola had taken her a hot drink up to bed, 'and satisfy myself that I can entrust you to him.'

Nicola had promised to produce Paul the following day—Saturday—and had spent a sleepless night wondering how to arrange it all. She was determined that her beloved Gran shouldn't be done out of her trip. After all, she was over seventy and nobody knew when she would have the chance to arrange it again, as the relatives in Melbourne were about to move to take over a ranch up-country.

Somehow, Nicola had vowed, she was going to fix it. Then, this morning, it had seemed to fix itself. Paul had rung to invite her to a party in the grounds of his mother's home. She could explain the situation and ask him to come home with her and meet Gran and be introduced as Nicola's fiancé, although she had no intention of holding him to his proposal. Once Gran had got on to the plane their 'engagement' would be at an end.

Paul would agree, she was sure. He was a good sport and he'd help her out, especially when he knew she wasn't taking his rash proposal seriously. So everyone would be happy. The train was drawing into the platform now and as Nicola jumped down she kept her fingers crossed, hoping things would turn out as she had planned.

She looked up and down the platform but Paul was nowhere to be seen. There were only two or three weary-looking businessmen with bulging briefcases approaching from the first-class end of the train. Of course, Paul would be waiting outside in his car.

She went through the booking office, giving up her ticket—single, of course, because she intended Paul to drive her home. That was all part of the plan.

'You're sure he'll bring you home?' Gran had worried. 'I couldn't bear to think of you crossing London alone at night.'

She'd laughed Gran's fears away. 'Of course I'm sure. When I get home tonight, I'll be officially engaged. I might even be wearing a ring.'

Out in the station yard she stopped. No BMW waiting for her. The only car drawn up at the kerb was a taxi, the driver deep in the racing results in the evening paper, a cigarette lolling from his mouth.

The businessmen all passed her, walking towards the car park, talking together and glancing with interest at the tall girl in a simple linen dress that matched her wonderful blue eyes. They looked away quickly; Dunton Green wasn't the kind of district where you encountered wolf-whistles. A few minutes later there was the sound of powerful engines starting up and cars leaving the park one by one. The ticket-collector went into his office and slammed the door.

Nicola was beginning to feel faintly annoyed. Was this a subtle ploy on Paul's part? It wouldn't be beyond him to calculate that if he kept her waiting it might sap her confidence so that he could move in for the kill more easily. Oh, no, she thought. Last night you asked me to marry you, whether you really meant it seriously or not, so I'm the one to make the next move.

The sun had set some time ago and there was only a faint pinkish-grey haze remaining behind the cupressus hedge that bordered the car park. A sneaky little breeze blew through the booking office and found its way into the gap between Nicola's frilly collar and the upward curve of her hair. She shivered, drew Gran's lace shawl around her and began to pace up and down impatiently. What should she do? Go back home? Disturb the solitary taxi man from his racing results and tell him to drive her to the Jarretts' home? She knew the name of the house, Pemberley Manor, although she'd never been there.

She decided on the latter course, but before she could reach the taxi a silver-grey Rolls-Royce glided into the yard and drew up beside her.

A chauffeur in grey uniform got out and touched his cap. 'Miss Oldfield? Mr Paul is sorry he couldn't get away in time to meet your train, miss. He's waiting for you at the house.'

He held open the rear door of the Rolls and Nicola got inside. This was a nuisance, because she'd planned to use the drive from the station to the house to explain her plan to Paul, but there was no help for it.

'Nice evening they've got for the party,' the chauffeur chatted as they drove through the quiet village and along the undulating pine-wooded roads.

'Yes, lovely,' Nicola agreed absently. She was deep in thought. What if he really had meant what he said last night, if he considered them engaged? It didn't seem likely but it was just possible. And if he did he might have told his mother. The other guests might be speculating about her... Whatever he intended she *must* get him alone as soon as she could.

The Rolls turned in between high stone gateposts, crunched down a long gravel drive bordered by shrubs and pulled up before an imposing mansion of mellow brick. Large glossy cars were parked all round the forecourt—there must have been quite twenty of them.

Now for it! Nicola nerved herself for what was to come.

As the chauffeur opened the car door for her Paul came running down the steps from the front door. He really was very good-looking, she thought, tallish and lithe, with crinkly golden hair and laughing brown eyes. He wasn't laughing now; in fact he looked distinctly nervous.

'Nicola—hello, glad you could make it.' He put a hand on her shoulder and dropped a quick kiss on her hair. He turned to the chauffeur. 'You can put the car away now, Steve. Mama won't be needing it any more to-night.' He linked his arm with Nicola's and hurried up the steps into a large tiled hall. An ornate antique table stood in the centre and the walls were hung with oil paintings in heavy gilt frames.

This was where Nicola must say her piece, but he didn't give her a chance. 'So sorry I couldn't meet your train,' he rattled on. 'There are always such a lot of odds and ends to see to at a do like this and Mama seems to look on me as an odd-job man. You'd better leave your shawl; you won't be needing it in the garden—it's stifling hot out there.' He opened a door and almost pushed her into a blue-tiled cloakroom.

Nicola added her shawl to the pile of elegant flimsy wraps hanging over the backs of chairs, took a quick look at herself in a gilt-framed mirror and joined Paul outside the door.

She tried again. 'Paul, there's something I want to say before...'

She might not have spoken. 'The food's outside.' He put a hand at her waist and propelled her through a garden-room, and through a glass door on to a long patio. 'Let's get out there before the guests eat everything. I'm starving and I'm sure you must be. Have you had anything to eat since lunch?'

Nicola made one last effort. She hung back. 'Really I...'

But he put a finger over her lips. 'Don't be nervous, sweetheart. I don't know any of the folk here either; they're mostly Mama's buddies. Come along.'

Nicola sighed and gave it up. They were on the lawn now, among the guests. She'd let Paul get her something to eat, and then she'd explain to him that they must get away alone to talk. She looked around her. Fairy-lamps winked from the tall poplars and guests stood about in groups, laughing and talking, or sat at the small tables waiting for their share of the feast. Two uniformed maids moved among the group of guests with laden trays. Music drifted softly from somewhere on the patio. The women's outfits were expensively casual and Nicola's pretty chain-store dress couldn't compete but at least Paul needn't feel ashamed of her. Not that that mattered; she didn't intend to make this a social occasion.

'Ah, there's Mama,' Paul said. 'Come and meet her.' He urged her along to the gazebo, where a thin woman was giving orders to one of the maids. The maid moved away and Paul pushed Nicola forward.

'Mama, this is Nicola Oldfield. I told you about her.'

Mrs Jarrett held out a cool hand, smiling formally. She seemed to be in her mid-fifties and had obviously taken care of her figure. She was elegantly dressed in a black crêpe de Chine trouser-suit with a wide filigree silver belt and long silver earrings. Rather over-dressed for a simple party, Nicola couldn't help thinking.

'How nice of Paul to bring you, Nicola,' she cooed in a high hostessy voice. 'We must see that you have a pleasant evening.'

'Thank you,' Nicola murmured. It wasn't turning out very pleasant so far, she thought grimly.

Mrs Jarrett's eyes ranged over her guests dotted about the lawn. 'Paul, darling, Colonel and Mrs O'Brien don't seem to have anything to drink. Do see to it, there's a good boy.'

Obediently, Paul disappeared into the crowd of guests with what Nicola thought was rather unseemly haste. It was almost as if he was anxious to get away from her.

Mrs Jarrett led the way to the rear of the gazebo and sat down on a wooden bench. She patted the place beside her. 'Come and sit here, Nicola, and we can have a little talk.'

Nicola's heart sank. This could only mean that Paul had taken the engagement seriously and had broken the news to his mother, who would doubtless not be pleased. A mere secretary would hardly be a suitable match for a director of Jarrett and Sons of London, one of the oldest and most highly respected wine importers in the country.

Nicola sat very straight and endured a lengthy inspection from the pale grey eyes of the woman beside her. Then, suddenly, Mrs Jarrett smiled and her rather hard face softened. 'You really are an exceptionally pretty girl, Nicola. I can quite understand why my son values your services so much, if your work as a secretary is equally impeccable, which I'm sure it is.'

'I do my best,' Nicola said rather stiffly. This really was an absurd situation.

Mrs Jarrett put out a hand and pressed Nicola's. 'Don't be angry with me, my dear; I'm not trying to patronise you. I'm just afraid that what I have to say may be rather hurtful and I don't like hurting people.'

Nicola put in, 'I think I know what you're going to say and I must...'

'Please, my dear, just listen first. Paul is like me. He's very sensitive and he, too, hates hurting people. He's asked me to explain to you that he may have given you a wrong impression. He's rather impulsive, as I'm sure you know, having worked with him, but he understands that he has several years yet of making his way up in the firm until the time comes to settle down. He'll be away in France for the next two weeks and we both think that this is the best time to make a break.'

This was incredible. Paul had asked his mother to do his dirty work for him. Nicola was almost speechless. Anger began to boil up inside her. 'To make a break? With me?' she said stiffly.

'Well, yes, that's what it amounts to.' Mrs Jarrett's mouth twitched with what might have been sympathy. 'We'll find you another little job, of course, and see that your salary isn't reduced.'

Nicola's knees were shaking so much that she could hardly stand up, but somehow she managed it. She had to hold on to her control for a few minutes more. 'Could we get this quite clear, Mrs Jarrett? Do you mean that Paul himself has asked you to—to intervene on his behalf?'

Mrs Jarrett nodded ruefully. 'The dear boy's so sensitive.'

'Yes, isn't he?' Nicola looked straight at the older woman, who had got to her feet now. 'Well, thank you for telling me this, Mrs Jarrett. I'll go and speak to Paul and then I must be leaving. It was good of you to invite me.'

Mrs Jarrett seemed less tall than she had a few minutes ago and her eyes were fixed on Nicola with a relieved expression in them. Probably she had expected tears or even hysterical pleading.

Nicola searched the groups of guests to find Paul. She would tell him exactly what she thought of him and then go home. But Paul was nowhere to be seen. She crossed the patio and into the garden-room. He wasn't there either. Paul was keeping out of her way, as well he might, she thought furiously. Well, there was only one thing to do. She would collect her shawl from the cloakroom and get away from this hateful place where she had been so humiliated, as quickly as she could, even if it meant walking to the station.

In the hall she tried to remember which was the door to the cloakroom. This one, she thought. She was wrong. The door opened into a large room which looked like a study, with books around the wall and high-backed wing-chairs in front of an inglenook fireplace.

She was about to close the door again when something hit her foot with a sharp rap that made her gasp. She looked down to see a golf ball resting against her white sandal. An elderly man, balding and comfortably tubby in a purple velvet jacket, approached her across an expanse of red Turkey carpet.

'Oh, dear, oh, dear, a very bad putt, I'm afraid. I hope I haven't maimed you, young lady.' He sounded too nice to belong to this household.

'Of course not.' Nicola picked up the ball and handed it back to him. 'I'm sorry I disturbed you.' She turned to go out of the room but the elderly man stopped her.

'Not a bit of it! Come in and talk to me, then I shall have an alibi for not joining in my daughter's festivities in the garden.' Nicola must have looked doubtful, for he added, 'Were you looking for someone? Can I be of any assistance——?'

'Well, yes, I was looking for Paul. I can't find him out in the garden. But really I mustn't trouble you.'

'No trouble at all. You're doing me a kindness, my dear. I was getting very bored with my own company. Now that I've retired from the firm the family thinks that I should take up a hobby, but something tells me that golf isn't going to be my game.' He smiled wryly and his wrinkled face looked benevolent and humorous. 'Whom do I have the pleasure of addressing?'

'My name's Oldfield,' Nicola said. 'Nicola Oldfield.'

He shook her hand cordially. 'Delighted to make your acquaintance, Miss Oldfield. Now, you sit yourself down and I'll go and find my grandson Paul for you. I'm not surprised you lost him; this house is like a rabbit warren.'

He padded out of the room and Nicola sank into the depths of one of the huge wing-chairs before the fireplace. She felt as if she was getting smaller and smaller every moment. Tears of sheer frustration began to prick behind her eyes and the colours of the flowers in the pottery vase standing in the hearth blurred together. Not only had she been humiliated, but there was no possibility now of enlisting Paul's help with the plan which meant so much to her. She had banked on his falling in with her idea, but now she wouldn't ask Paul Jarrett for anything. She wouldn't ask him for a drink if she were dying of thirst in the desert, she told herself dramatically.

Suddenly the door opened behind her and she sank deeper into the chair, wiping her eyes with her handkerchief. If Paul saw her weeping he would put all the wrong constructions on it. The first thing she heard was Paul's voice. 'Pour me a stiff one, there's a good chap.' He couldn't be speaking to his grandfather, surely? He went

on, 'I've got to face Nicola now that Mama's done her
stuff, and I'm not looking forward to it. I feel a heel
about ditching her.'

A deep, amused voice said, 'But then, you *are* rather
a heel, aren't you, chum?'

Nicola tried to stand up, but her legs didn't seem to
be functioning. She just had to hope that when the two
men had had their drinks they'd go away.

The deep voice said, 'There you are—half and half.
That's strong enough for you. We don't want your mama
to think her golden boy has been naughty again, do we?'

'Oh, shut up, and stop needling me,' came Paul's
voice. 'Whatever you think I really do feel bad about
Nicola. Last night...' he swallowed noisily '...I truly
believed I was in love with her.'

'A fairly frequent delusion of yours, old boy,' was the
mocking reply.

'Oh, *you*! I know your views on the subject. You don't
know what it's like to fall in love.'

'I sincerely hope not,' was the mocking reply. 'I gather
from looking around that love is a commodity that com-
plicates life quite unacceptably.'

Nicola's hands clenched. Who was this utter, utter
swine that Paul was talking to?

The deep voice cut in abruptly, 'Are you sleeping with
her?'

'No,' admitted Paul sulkily. 'That's why...'

'Why you dangled the marriage thing before her eyes,
I suppose, and then got cold feet when you woke up this
morning and realised what you'd done. And then were
feeble enough to enlist your mama's help to extricate
you—not for the first time, I imagine.'

Paul flared up. 'That's a rotten thing to say. Why the
holier-than-thou attitude? Don't tell me you've never
wanted to take a girl to bed.'

A brief laugh. 'Be your age, Paul. But at least I don't have to dangle a wedding-ring as bait. Have you made up your mind what you're going to do with this girl—Nicola, is it?'

'Do with her?'

'Yes, she's been working as your secretary, hasn't she? It won't be a good idea to keep her on after this little—er—débâcle, will it? And I shouldn't think she'd want to stay on, if she's got any spirit. What will you do, throw her back into the typing pool like a netted fish? Yes, I see, you haven't given it a thought. You really are a bastard, Paul. And has it occurred to you what the outcome may be? Remember the old adage "a woman scorned"? Do you want to drag the family name into the gutter if she goes round crying rape, or sells her story to the tabloids?' The deep voice had a cutting edge now.

'Don't be silly.' Paul's voice trembled ever so slightly. 'Nicola wouldn't—she's a nice girl; she's not like that.'

A cynical laugh. 'You really are an infant, Paul. Haven't you learned yet that all girls are like that? On the make? Well, you'd better decide what you're going to do before she comes looking for you.'

There was a groan from Paul. 'Oh, hell—hell—hell—what a mess! What *am* I going to say to her, Saul?'

Saul! Ah, now she knew who the other man was. Saul Jarrett, the chairman and managing director of the company, who inhabited rooms on the top floor, and was hardly ever seen in the general office. Well, she was going to see him now at close quarters. Her legs moved without her willing them. She emerged from behind the big chair and faced the two men on the other side of the room. 'It won't be necessary for you to say anything, Paul,' she said calmly. 'You've said it all.' Her eyes passed from Paul to the other man, leaning nonchalantly against the bookcase, glass in hand, amusement written large on his dark, sardonic face.

'Nicola!' Paul's cheeks were bright red. He looked as if he was about to burst into tears. He took a step towards her. 'I didn't—I wouldn't...'

'You have,' Nicola said quietly. She stood up straight in her pretty flowery dress. Her satin-smooth hair, tipped up at the ends, gave her white face an almost stern look, like Joan of Arc preparing for battle.

'I don't intend to apologise for eavesdropping,' she went on, 'because from the first few words I knew I was going to hear the truth, straight from the horse's mouth.' She gave Paul a very direct look and added, 'Or perhaps I should say from the rabbit's mouth.'

She heard a guffaw from the direction of the bookcase but she didn't turn her head. 'There's nothing more to be said. If someone would ring for a taxi to take me to the station I'd be grateful.'

'Of course. I'll drive you myself,' Paul began weakly but the other man suddenly detached himself from the bookcase.

He was even taller than he had seemed at first—taller and darker now that he stood under the light. He towered above Paul. His eyes were dark slits, glinting beneath thick curved lashes, and the hollows in his cheeks gave his face a gaunt, hungry look. His shoulders were wide under their tailored cloth. There was an air about him which proclaimed him the dominant male in any situation.

Nicola shivered slightly. She wouldn't like to tangle with *him*, she thought, and a ripple of something like fear ran down behind her ribs.

He looked down at Paul, his long mouth curling. 'OK, cousin,' he said, 'your part in this little drama is over. I still have a few lines to deliver so I'll drive Nicola home.

Come along, Nicola, have you a coat or wrap to rescue? We'll make our exit through the side-door—that'll avoid the crush.'

Nicola didn't feel capable of arguing. Anyway, one look at the man was enough to convince her that it would be futile. He had made up his mind, and that was that. But no way was she going to let him drive her all the way home. She could put up with him as far as the station and no further. She would insist upon his dropping her there.

She held her head high. 'Thank you,' she said, and walked with him out of the room without another look at Paul.

CHAPTER TWO

SAUL JARRETT'S car was one of the glossy monsters parked in the driveway. He installed Nicola in the front, pulled off his jacket, threw it on the back seat and got in beside her, slamming the door. All his movements seemed to suggest a barely concealed impatience. Obviously he wasn't relishing having this unpleasant task wished upon him.

As they fastened their seatbelts his arm brushed against hers and to Nicola's horror she felt an unmistakable stirring, an instinctive response to his body-warmth, reaching her bare arm through the thin stuff of his shirt. She drew away quickly. She hadn't met a man who touched a sexual chord in her since the affair with Keith, and that had ended two years ago. Of course, Saul Jarrett was the dark, brooding type who attracted women effortlessly—but he had no possible interest for her, she assured herself. He would drive her to the station and that would be the last she'd see of him. And a good thing too, she thought sourly.

As soon as they were out on the road he said abruptly, 'Where's home?'

'Oh, if you'll just drop me off at the station that'll suit me fine,' she told him hastily.

'Where's home?' he repeated wearily, as if she hadn't spoken.

Rude brute, Nicola thought, and said, 'Watford.' That should be far enough away to put him off the idea of driving her home.

'Watford? And how do you propose to get there?'

'Easily. Train, tube, train, then it's only a few minutes' walk.'

They were on the outskirts of the village now and the car slowed down to keep to the speed limit, but passed the British Rail sign to the station without turning in.

'That,' said Saul crushingly, 'is the most idiotic itinerary I've ever heard. You don't imagine I'd let you wander round London at night on your own, do you?'

'Why not?' she said, ignoring the dictatorial note in his voice. 'And I don't intend to "wander round" London,' she said edgily.

'No, and I don't intend to allow you to. You're much too eye-catching in that pretty dress.'

Flattery now? He must have remembered that she might make things difficult for Paul and put a blot on the stainless name of Jarrett and Sons.

'I know Watford quite well,' he said. 'What's the address?'

It was no good arguing with the man and she was beginning to feel tired. She told him the address and he grunted with satisfaction. 'Yes, I know exactly where that is. Now, I've got an idea. There's quite a decent road-house a little further on. We'll stop there and have something to eat.'

'I'm not...'

'Hungry? Well, I am. I haven't had a bite since breakfast and I'll drive much more safely with some food inside me. Because I intend to drive you home, you know, Miss——? I'm afraid I don't recall your other name.'

'Oldfield.' She might as well accept gracefully because he would simply ignore any protests in his high-handed way. Besides, the Jarrett family owed her a meal before she left the firm—and nothing would persuade her to stay on now.

The road-house was clean and bright. The sausages were grilled to a turn, the chips were crisp and golden. Nicola surprised herself by feeling hungry. She asked for Perrier to drink and Saul joined her—as he was driving, he remarked. That fitted his persona, Nicola thought with amusement, as a man of high principles.

The meal finished with coffee and after-dinner mints and then they went back to the car.

'Thank you,' Nicola said politely. 'I enjoyed that.'

Beyond a few casual remarks there had been no conversation during the meal. There was nothing to say, was there? Saul Jarrett was merely saving the family honour by driving her home, and that suited Nicola.

'Good,' he said and opened the car door for her.

She was inside in a flash and fastened her seatbelt before there was any danger of their arms touching. When he was settled he slipped a cassette into the stereo and the pleasant sound of Mozart filled the car. Saul sat back, completely relaxed, humming the melody as he drove, with complete confidence, through the increasingly heavy traffic—over the river, straight through the centre of London, and then northwards.

Nicola stared out of the window and the lights blurred before her eyes as she worried about what she was going to tell Gran when she got home. It was going to be such a horrid disappointment if Gran had to cancel her holiday, but she knew Gran. She had a resolute will under her sweetly amiable exterior and she wasn't going to budge over anything that seemed to involve Nicola's safety and well-being.

When her daughter and son-in-law were killed in a car crash, on their way home from a concert—a celebration of their tenth wedding anniversary—it had never occurred to Gran not to take early retirement from her job as headmistress of a junior school, so that she could

devote her life to bringing up the two-year-old Nicola.
Which she had done, with loving care, and a modicum
of discipline, for the following twenty years.

As the car drove further out of London Nicola began
to recognise landmarks and knew they were nearing
Watford and her spirits sank lower and lower. Oh, damn,
damn, damn, why did this have to happen just now of
all times? How could she remove herself from the threat
of danger? She knew nobody sufficiently well to suggest
parking herself on them for a month's stay. A hotel?
But that would cost the earth and Gran would never
agree. Miserable and frustrated, Nicola wiped her eyes
and blew her nose hard.

At the same moment Saul turned the car into a side-
road and stopped beside a row of railings which suggested
a park or a cemetery behind them. The light from a
street-lamp filtered through the leaves of a tree, just
ahead.

He switched off the engine and Nicola's head jerked
round. What was he up to? Surely, surely, he wasn't
going to make a pass at her, not after all that had happened. He couldn't be as crass as that.

He was lying back in his corner and in the flickering
light from the street-lamp she could see that his black
eyes were half closed, regarding her fixedly. 'Paul isn't
worth your tears, you know,' he said, and she felt relieved that there was no innuendo in the deep voice.
'Were you *very* disappointed?'

'Of course I was,' she said shortly. Any other reply
would have been too complicated to explain. And it was
true, of course. She *was* very disappointed—but not because of Paul's behaviour. She'd almost forgotten about
Paul already.

'What do you propose to do, Miss Oldfield?'

'Do? Do about what?'

'I was thinking of your future plans.' Did he sound faintly uneasy, or was it her imagination?

'Well, I don't much care for the idea of being thrown back into the typing pool like a netted fish,' she said tartly. She waited for that to sink in and then she added, 'In fact, I'd never work for Jarrett and Sons again.'

'Yes,' he said slowly. 'I was afraid you'd take that view of the company, and it's a view that I don't like at all. We think a great deal of our good name and I like to believe that we at Jarretts have a reputation for treating our staff fairly in all circumstances. This is somewhat outside the way of business, of course, but still——' He reached to an inside pocket and drew out a cheque-book and gold-plated pen.

Nicola stared incredulously at the cheque-book and the pen held poised above it expectantly. Was there to be no end to the indignity she was suffering from the Jarrett family?

'Are you thinking of buying me off, Mr Jarrett?' she said icily.

'Buying you off? What are you talking about? I merely thought I might be of some practical help to tide you over until you find another job.'

'You're quite sure you weren't thinking of putting me off the idea of approaching the tabloids with some nice juicy scandal story about one of your directors?' she said with saccharine sweetness.

There was a silence and she knew she'd scored a hit. She went on, 'I don't want your money, Mr Jarrett, and I consider that you're adding insult to humiliation by offering it to me.'

He shrugged and replaced the cheque-book. 'Whatever you say.' He sounded icily cold now and very weary of the whole situation. He straightened up in his seat. 'Well, let me know if I can be of assistance to you in any way.'

'Wait a minute,' Nicola said sharply as his hand went to the ignition. An idea had suddenly flashed into her mind. It was a wild idea, a very long shot, but it was worth a try. 'You did say in any way at all, didn't you?' she asked.

'Any way within reason.' He was patronising her, thinking of references, personal contacts, no doubt.

'To safeguard the reputation of the firm of Jarrett?' She couldn't resist adding a touch of malice to the words.

'Well?' he said suspiciously.

She swallowed and plunged in. 'Are you married, Mr Jarrett?'

'Heaven forbid!' he burst out, surprised out of his usual careful consideration of his words. Then he recovered his *sang-froid*. 'I trust you're not suggesting that I should step into my cousin's shoes as your fiancé?' he drawled, his voice dripping with irony.

Nicola felt like a gambler who had put every last penny on one final throw of the dice. She said smoothly, 'As a matter of fact, that *is* what I was going to suggest.'

There was a second's tense silence. Then, '*What*?' he roared, his fury filling the car.

Nicola felt fear curl in her stomach. She'd hoped rather vaguely that he'd laugh at her apparently outrageous suggestion, so that they could talk. It would have meant that he wasn't totally arrogant and cynical. But evidently she'd credited him with a sense of humour he didn't possess.

'I didn't mean...' she faltered.

'Get out of the car, you little slut! You can find your own way home.' He leaned across her roughly and flung open the passenger door.

Really frightened now, Nicola edged away and put one foot over the sill. She turned back. 'Please listen...'

'Go on, get out,' he yelled.

She stumbled. Her other foot caught in the sill. She lost her balance and pitched forward into the road.

She tried to stand up but her head was swimming and she fell back again. The throb of the engine sounded close to her ears. Was he going to drive away and leave her lying here? She almost hoped he would.

But instead she was aware of his dark form looming over her. 'What's the matter—are you hurt?'

'Go away,' she screamed hysterically. 'Leave me alone.'

She touched her forehead and her fingers encountered something sticky. She was dying—that man had killed her.

'Don't move,' he ordered and she felt his hands on her, on her legs, her arms. Then he touched her forehead and she let out a howl.

'My God!' he muttered, but his hands felt gentle as they pushed her heavy hair away from her face. Then she felt a soft pad pressing gently over the wound.

He was too near. Her arms flailed about uselessly, trying to push him away.

'Keep still, can't you?' he shouted angrily and he lifted her bodily and put her back into the car.

Nicola stared at the street-lamp above her head. It began to revolve very slowly, then lurched, stopped, and turned the other way. Nausea rose inside her. She concentrated every bit of will-power she had left on not being sick. The man beside her was talking but she couldn't make out what he was saying. After that she didn't know anything at all.

Everything was quiet and still. The car must have stopped. Nicola opened her eyes cautiously. A hundred little men with road-drills were hammering into her head.

She turned her head a fraction and saw, in the dim light, Gran's face watching her anxiously. She was in her own bed at home. Oh, blessed relief!

'What happened?' she whispered.

'Shh, dear, don't try to talk.' Gran's voice, kind as always. 'You've had a nasty tumble but you'll soon be all right. The doctor's seen you and he says you'll be as right as rain in two or three days. He wants you to take these tablets.'

Hazy memories of childhood illnesses floated into Nicola's mind. And of Gran, always cheerful, and loving, and optimistic.

Childhood habits persisted and Nicola had been a good child. Now she opened her mouth obediently and Gran popped the two tablets in and held a glass of water to her lips. She choked on the tablets but at last she managed to get them down. 'Ugh!' She tried to smile at Gran but the familiar face kept coming and going in the most peculiar way.

There was something—something important. Oh, yes, she remembered now. 'You mustn't—miss—your flight, Gran,' she muttered.

Gran patted her hand gently. 'Of course I shan't; it's all arranged. Now you have a nice long sleep and don't worry.' Gratefully, Nicola closed her eyes and did as she was told.

When she wakened again the sun was making bright edging to the blue curtains. Nicola lay still, looking at the ceiling. The pain in her head had quietened to a dull ache, and gradually she began to piece together memories of the previous night. The party—the scene in the study—the car drive... She shivered as everything became suddenly clear. That horrible man—she didn't want to remember.

She heard the door open and smiled, turning her head very carefully as Gran came towards the bed.

'Gran——' she began, and stopped dead.

It wasn't the face of her beloved Gran that was looking down at her. It was the dark, inscrutable face of Saul Jarrett.

Nicola tried to scream but no sound came. It was like a nightmare. She turned her head on the pillow, away from the gaze of those liquid black eyes. She tried to shout, Go away, but it came out as a croak.

'It's all right, you needn't be afraid. I'm not going to hurt you.' His voice was deep, even, completely unemotional.

'Where's Gran? I want Gran.'

'Gran just went out to catch the shops before they close. She won't be long. She left tea ready to make. She said you'd want some when you woke up. Now you just lie quiet and I'll bring it up to you.' He went out of the room.

It was no use trying to think, to sort out what was happening. Perhaps her mind would begin to work when she'd had some tea.

She heard a clatter in the kitchen below, and very soon Saul was back with a tray.

He put it down on the dressing-table, pushing aside the pots and bottles. 'I brought an extra cup for myself,' he remarked. 'How do you like it—milk, sugar?'

'Milk, no sugar.' She wouldn't say 'please'. She owed this man no courtesy—he'd tried to kill her. Well, not exactly kill, perhaps, but that was what might have happened.

He poured out a cup of tea and put it beside her on the bedside table. She pulled herself up in the bed. Every movement hurt but she wasn't going to appear in need of help. She really would die if he touched her, she thought dramatically.

She gulped down the tea and eyed Saul, who had drawn up a chair and was sitting beside the bed, balancing his teacup. He looked very much at home.

Nicola gathered her strength. 'I want to know why you're here. What you're doing in my home, making tea, speaking of my grandmother as if you were one of our family.'

He finished the tea before he replied. Then he said, 'Well, I suppose I am, in a way. As your fiancé.'

'My fiancé?' she gasped.

He went on evenly, in that deep, controlled voice which seemed to be having a faintly hypnotic effect on Nicola, 'That was what you wanted, wasn't it? What you were going to suggest when I so impolitely threw you out of my car? That I should pose as your fiancé, so that your grandmother wouldn't have to cancel her trip to Australia on account of the danger to you if she left you alone here?'

Nicola put her cup down and sank back against the pillows. 'What are you?' she said weakly. 'Do you carry a crystal ball around with you?'

'I didn't need one. When I brought you home last night your Gran addressed me as Paul and took it for granted that you and I were engaged. With you lying unconscious in my arms it hardly seemed the moment for explanations. We needed to get a doctor to you— quickly. Fortunately he was at home and I brought him back with me. It was a great relief when he could find no physical injury except the wound on your head. He thought you would soon recover consciousness and he left tablets for you to take to make you sleep. All of which happened as he expected. When you were duly

asleep Gran and I had a long talk. I think she quite took
to me,' he added with beastly smugness.

'I suppose you invented some story to account for the
accident?' Nicola enquired. 'She wouldn't like you very
much if she knew the truth.'

'She might understand if she knew the whole story,'
he said calmly, 'and how you deliberately provoked me.
A man can only take so much,' he added. 'After that
he must protect himself, even if it means using—er—
ungentlemanly behaviour.'

Nicola closed her eyes wearily. 'I don't know what
you mean.'

'Don't you? Don't you really? How old are you,
Nicola?'

'Twenty-two,' she said.

There was a short pause. 'I thought every girl...' he
began, then added in the ironic tone she'd begun to
know, 'You must have led a very sheltered life.'

She hadn't the strength to argue with him.

He sat back in his chair. 'Well,' he said at last. 'What's
it to be? I'm prepared to act as your fiancé for the
moment, so that your gran's plans need not be changed.
She told me how you had to persuade her to go in the
first instance, but I believe she very much wants to see
her family in Melbourne, and that another chance may
not come along for some time.'

Nicola eyed the dark, impassive face curiously. 'I'd
like to know why you're making this offer. Surely not
out of the goodness of your heart?'

He smiled without humour. 'Oh, no, my heart doesn't
prompt me to make altruistic gestures. No, it's a matter
of conscience. I feel that my family hasn't treated you
very well, and I should like to set the record straight.'

'I see,' Nicola said slowly. She thought for a moment
or two. Then she said, 'Very well, I accept your offer—

as a business arrangement. I very much want my grand-mother to have her holiday; she deserves it. She's been wonderful to me.' She didn't realise that her voice was soft and her deep blue eyes suddenly glowed with tenderness.

'We're agreed, then,' the man said abruptly. 'I'll try to play my part convincingly.'

The ache in Nicola's head was beginning to get worse. Thinking was too much trouble. She laid her head back and closed her eyes and there was silence in the room. She hoped Saul would go away now but he still sat there, not speaking. Then the front door closed and Gran's steps sounded on the stairs.

Nicola opened her eyes and smiled as Gran came into the room. She was carrying an enormous bunch of roses, swathed in florist's wrapping paper. Gran looked from Saul, sitting beside the bed, to Nicola's white face. 'You've wakened up, dear. You've had a lovely sleep; how are you feeling?'

'Much better, thanks, Gran. I'll get up later on.'

'Oh, no.' Gran and the man beside the bed both spoke at once. Then Gran went on firmly, 'The doctor said two days' rest in bed.'

Saul Jarrett added, 'As a precaution against concussion.'

Gran put the flowers into Saul's hands. 'These were the best I could find,' she said. 'They hadn't any red ones.'

'Thank you, Gran, I'm most grateful.' He smiled quite winningly at Gran. So he could smile! But not at her, of course, Nicola thought.

But she was quite wrong. He turned to her with an even more charming smile, and the black eyes were shining. 'For you, darling,' he said. 'With my love.'

He leaned down. Heavens, he was going to kiss her. Nicola's whole body stiffened as his lips came down to hers. This was something she had to put up with if they were going to reassure Gran, and she hated the deceit. All in a good cause, she encouraged herself, and kept her mouth tightly closed.

But Saul wasn't going to settle for a token kiss. He bit her lower lip quite gently but it was enough to make her open her mouth a little way, and then the kiss deepened. As his tongue found hers a tremor ran through her and her body relaxed its tense resistance. She heard Saul's quick intake of breath and then his hand closed over her breast. Her pulses jumped and her back arched itself involuntarily. Her arms went up round Saul's neck and she drew him closer.

Suddenly she realised what he must think of her. 'Is that convincing enough?' she whispered in his ear. She wasn't going to let him think he had actually disturbed her if she could help it. His lips were warm on her neck.

'For the moment,' he whispered back, and that sounded horribly like a promise. What did it mean? Was he intending to pay her out for landing him in this situation? If he was he could think again. Once Gran was safely on her plane Saul Jarrett could fade out of the picture.

Saul straightened himself and Nicola saw that Gran had moved away tactfully and was looking out of the window.

'And now I'm horribly afraid I must leave you,' he said with apparent reluctance as Gran turned and came back to the bed. 'I can't tell you how relieved I am, my darling——' he cast a fond glance at Nicola '—to find you on the road to recovery. I was prepared to cancel my business trip to Paris, but as things are I suppose I'd better go. Gran will look after you beautifully and I'll phone every day for the doctor's progress report.'

Nicola was only half listening. That kiss had shattered what little composure she had left.

'I'll make a point of being back by Thursday,' Saul was saying, 'in plenty of time to take you to Heathrow for your flight on Friday. By which time I hope you'll be well enough to come too, Nicola, dear. Now, I must go—*au revoir*, my sweet.' He kissed Nicola again, briefly this time.

'I'll see you off,' Gran said. She picked up the flowers and led the way downstairs.

She was back again before Nicola had had time to gather her chaotic thoughts together. She had a strong suspicion that it was she who had been tricked into this absurd situation and not Saul, but she couldn't have said why, and anyway the end result was that Gran's trip was going to be secured.

Gran put the vase of pink roses down near Nicola on the bedside table. 'There! Aren't they beautiful? Saul asked me to go out and get them because he wanted to be here when you wakened up. He wouldn't leave until he was quite sure that you'd really come round.'

'You mean—he's been here all night?'

'Yes, we took it in turns to stay with you.' Gran perched on the edge of the bed. 'It's been a very traumatic way to get to know your future husband, Nicola, love, but in a crisis people get to know each other very quickly and I'm sure you couldn't have chosen a better man. He's been wonderful.'

Nicola murmured something which might have been an expression of pleasure. She supposed she must begin to play her part in the charade that she and Saul had just agreed to. It shouldn't be too difficult if he was going to be away for the next few days, and she would only have to see him again for a short time when he arrived to take Gran to Heathrow. After that they could part with honour satisfied on his side and her own difficulty settled.

Gran was still going on about Saul. 'Once you were sound asleep last night we had time for a little talk over a cup of coffee. Poor man, he was nearly out of his mind when he got you home last night. He rushed out and fetched the doctor and insisted on bringing him back with him, and he was so relieved when the doctor said you'd be all right. He's very much in love with you, my dear.'

Ha! If only Gran knew the truth, Nicola thought, remembering the choice name he had called her last night.

'It was a mix-up at first,' Gran was rattling on. 'I got his name wrong. I thought you said Paul, not Saul. My hearing must be getting worse than I thought. He was so sympathetic when I told him about that horrid attack on the girl—they haven't caught the man yet, you know—and he quite understood that I couldn't possibly have gone away on Wednesday and left you all alone. He telephoned the travel agent this morning and arranged to change my flight to Friday, so all will fit in well. I'm sure you'll be quite yourself by then and well enough to come and see me off. But if you're not then Saul will stay with you and get his secretary to drive me to the airport and see me on to the plane.' She smiled. 'It's very useful to have plenty of money sometimes, isn't it? Especially when emergencies happen. And Saul is so thoughtful. He even insisted on ordering a taxi to take me to the shop to buy the flowers.' She sighed with pleasure and her cheeks were touched with pink as she got to her feet.

The wretched man had evidently put himself out to charm Gran and win her confidence, and he'd succeeded. She felt angry when she thought how Gran would be disappointed to hear that the 'engagement' had been called off. Nicola's head began to ache again when she wondered how she was going to keep up the pretence for the month Gran would be away, because that was what she would have to do. Oh, well, she would just have to play it by ear, she thought tiredly. She couldn't think any more now.

'I'll have another sleep now,' she told Gran, and Gran tidied up her pillows, put a glass of water beside the bed, drew the curtains closer together and tiptoed out of the room to go downstairs and plan a nice light supper for the patient when she was ready for it.

Nicola lay quiet, and the scent of the roses seemed to hang on the air round the bed. Saul had certainly entered into the spirit of the game, she thought wryly. That kiss—an involuntary little shudder passed over her. She hoped he wouldn't consider it necessary to kiss her like that very often.

Or—did she hope he would?

Stop it, you idiot, and forget the man. You know you hate him.

But as she drifted off to sleep she knew, in a hazy way, that whatever happened next Saul Jarrett wasn't going to be easy to forget.

CHAPTER THREE

NICOLA hated having to stay in bed for the next two days. Once the pain in her head had eased off she felt perfectly well, but Gran insisted on her obeying the doctor's orders to the letter. 'If you won't then I shan't leave on Friday,' she announced firmly. 'What if you developed concussion after I'd left? I couldn't risk leaving poor Saul to cope with that.'

'Poor Saul', Nicola thought wryly, would pack her off to hospital and that would be that. She had no illusions about Saul Jarrett. He would have salved his conscience and safeguarded the good name of his company, and would have no further interest in her.

She even doubted, as she lay in bed turning things over and over in her mind, whether he would reappear at all. He could say that he'd been detained in Paris and instruct his secretary to see Gran on to her plane. Yes, that was what he would do, she decided, and it would be a great relief not to have to see him again.

Now and again it occurred to her that she was spending all the time thinking of Saul, and then she reminded herself that he was the key to the whole problem of getting Gran safely away on her trip. Gran herself had no doubts about Saul, it seemed. She prided herself on being a good judge of character and sang his praises to Nicola until Nicola could have screamed. He was a fine man, a really good, kind man, and Nicola was a very lucky girl to be chosen by him. Gran, Nicola reflected, amusement mixed with irritation, still lived in an age when girls waited about meekly to be 'chosen'.

Certainly Saul was keeping his promise to phone from Paris each evening to enquire after Nicola. As there was no extension phone in the bedroom Gran took the calls and hurried up eagerly to tell Nicola exactly what he'd said. 'The dear boy is so glad you're progressing well. He said to give you his fondest love and say that he's longing to see you again on Friday morning, in time to go to the airport.'

Nicola tried to look thrilled. She thought sourly that he was overdoing the hearts-and-flowers touch and was thankful she didn't have to talk to him herself. By Wednesday she was sitting up in her room. The doctor was satisfied with her progress and on Thursday she came downstairs but she made sure she went to bed early before Saul's usual call came through.

But there was no call on Thursday. He was backing out, Nicola was sure of it. Gran said, 'I expect he's on his way home and can't get to a phone.' She didn't doubt for a moment that he would keep his promise and would turn up next morning.

On Thursday night Nicola slept badly and she was up and dressed and downstairs making coffee and toast by half-past six. She had no idea of the time of the flight. Either Saul hadn't told Gran, or she had forgotten. With implicit trust, which Nicola thought pathetic, Gran was leaving all the arrangements to Saul.

Nicola drank a cup of coffee and prowled round restlessly. In the hall Gran's luggage stood ready, her tweed coat neatly folded on top of the bulky travelling bag. Nicola had bought the lightweight bag as a present, when the invitation had first arrived, and she and Gran had spent hours planning and discussing what clothes would be suitable for a month's stay in Australia, in what would be winter over there. Looking at the bag they had packed together so hopefully, Nicola wanted to howl.

She went upstairs and found Gran finalising all the bits and pieces she would take in her in-flight bag. She was already wearing her little tweed hat pulled down firmly over her wiry grey hair. Her cheeks were pink with excitement.

'Good morning, dear; I'm almost ready in case Saul arrives early. I wish I could remember what time he said he'd be here.'

She popped two paperbacks and a wad of clean handkerchiefs in the bag and zipped it up. 'Isn't it exciting?' She gave Nicola a quick hug. 'Everything's turned out so well. You getting engaged, and Saul being such a dear boy. Just think, I might not be going at all. They haven't found that awful man yet, you know. It's frightening to think he may still be prowling around here. But we mustn't think of horrible things this morning, when you're so happy.'

Nicola couldn't take much more. 'There's coffee in the kitchen, Gran, and I made toast. I think you should have something to eat, you know. You go on down; I'll bring your bag.'

'Thanks, dear.' Gran trotted off downstairs.

Nicola sat down on the bed. How long would it be before it became clear that he wasn't coming? She glanced at her watch. It was a quarter-past eight. Another hour, she thought. If he hadn't come, or phoned, by then, that would be it. In spite of the evening phone calls from Paris, he would have decided, when it came to the point, not to go on with this charade. At first he would have been worried by her accident and the possibility that he might be blamed, but as the days passed and it was obvious that she was getting better he would have concluded that he needn't take any further part in the proceedings.

Gran had left her bedroom window open and Nicola went across to close it. As she did so she heard a phone ringing and jumped an inch in the air, her nerves taut as violin strings. But it was the phone next door.

She closed the window and locked it—out of habit, because they wouldn't be going anywhere.

Gran's room faced the front and Nicola looked idly up and down the road. The postman was cycling past, his letters delivered. The two boys from across the way were setting out for school early. Mrs Sugden's ginger cat jumped up on the wall of next door but one and began to wash himself carefully.

'Nicola!' Gran's voice called to her from below.

'Coming,' she called back, then as she turned away from the window her eye caught sight of a black car rounding the corner of the road. She stared, transfixed. It was slowing down. It had stopped outside their gate.

The front-door bell rang and Nicola was still glued to the spot, her heart jumping about crazily.

She heard voices in the hall, Gran's high and excited, then *his* voice, deep and velvety.

Nicola thought she was going to faint. She clung to the brass knob of Gran's old-fashioned bedstead until the swimmy feeling passed off. She heard Saul bounding up the stairs two at a time. 'Nicola, darling, how are you, my sweet?' This in a raised voice, for Gran's benefit. Then, in a low tone, 'What's the matter? You look terrible.'

She said the first thing that occurred to her. 'I thought you didn't mean to turn up.'

He gave her a hard look. 'You must understand, my girl, that when I undertake to do something I do it. And I intend to make sure that you do the same,' he added. Before she could make out what he meant by that he said briskly, 'Now, come along, hurry. I've had to cut the time very close. I'll get Gran into the car.' He ran down the stairs.

Nicola picked up Gran's hand luggage, grabbed a light coat from her own room, and followed him.

Several hours later Nicola stood beside Saul and watched the great plane taxi along the runway for the final turn. Its nose lifted and it rose slowly into the air. Higher and higher, faster and faster, engines roaring, until a few moments later the noise faded away and it had passed out of sight.

She let out her breath on a long sigh and her fingers unclenched themselves from her damp palms. It had actually happened. Until this moment she had hardly dared believe that it would.

Saul glanced down at her. 'Well, that's that,' he said with satisfaction. He looked a little closer. 'You look as if you could do with a large black coffee,' he said. 'Let's go and find one.'

She let him lead her through the milling Heathrow crowds to a coffee-shop. Here they sat down at a table with steaming mugs of coffee before them.

'Well,' said Saul, 'mission accomplished. Are you satisfied?'

Reaction was taking its toll. Nicola looked away from him, nodding without speaking.

'You've taken all this very seriously,' he said. 'Did it mean such a lot to you?'

She nodded, looking down into her coffee-mug. 'I'd set my heart on it, for Gran,' she said, 'and when I set my heart on something really worthwhile I do everything I can to make it come true.'

She looked up and met the dark eyes regarding her intently across the table. She wished he wouldn't look at her like that; it made her feel nervous.

'Even to the extent of proposing marriage to an almost complete stranger?' he said softly.

'I *didn't* propose marriage.' She almost shouted the words and then looked quickly round at the other tables, but nobody seemed to be listening.

'Sorry,' he drawled. 'I thought that was exactly what you did. You suggested I should take Paul's place, I seem to remember.'

Suddenly stung, she burst out crossly, 'I did no such thing; it was you yourself who put it like that. If you'd just listened to what I was going to say instead of man-handling me out of the car, you wouldn't have misun-derstood, and accused me of something—something horrible. I've no idea what.'

'Ah!' he drawled. 'Poor little girl! You haven't yet learned what a nasty world it is.'

'Don't patronise me,' she snapped, and drank her coffee up at a gulp.

'That's better,' Saul said, with maddening suavity. 'There's some colour in your cheeks now. I wondered if you were well enough to come to the airport this morning.'

'I'm fine,' she said. 'I couldn't have not come to see Gran off after—after...'

His dark brows rose a fraction. 'You didn't trust me? You thought I might kidnap the old lady, or put her on the plane to Timbuktu.'

She supposed that was his idea of a joke and she smiled feebly. 'Of course not. We couldn't have done without you. You've looked after everything for us and I'm very grateful. It would have been difficult for me; I'm not very experienced in air travel.'

'And Gran's never flown before, she told me. She's a gallant old lady.' Saul thought for a moment and then added, 'She wouldn't have consented to go if it hadn't been for our little—er—deception?'

'She certainly wouldn't,' Nicola said. She smiled fondly. 'Under Gran's sweet old lady exterior lies a firmness of purpose left over from her days as a nursery school head teacher. You need a good deal of firmness to keep twenty under-fives in order.'

She drank the rest of her coffee and put down the mug. 'Now, I must be getting home. We've taken up too much of your time already.' She gave him a fleeting smile. 'I hope that honour is satisfied. If you could just drop me at the station...'

His wide, mobile mouth twitched. 'What a girl you are for being dropped off at stations. You're not a railway fanatic, are you? No, Nicola, I have other plans. I have the day free and we'll drive straight back to Watford.'

He took her assent for granted. 'Come on, then, let's go,' he said, leading the way out of the coffee-room.

It was hot and crowded in the main hall. Saul took her arm to guide her through the throng but Nicola managed to slip out of his grasp. She had taken off her coat and the touch of his hard, dry hand on her bare arm made her shiver. As she followed him to the car park she remembered what he had said to Paul in the study—that he didn't have to dangle a wedding-ring in front of a girl to get her into his bed. She could believe that. She had to admit that he was a dangerously attractive man. It was just as well, she thought ruefully, that he obviously considered her a naïve little innocent, certainly not worth practising his charisma on. For some reason—pride, perhaps—she felt more angry than relieved.

When they were back in the car Saul consulted his watch. 'Nearly one,' he said. 'We won't fight our way into a restaurant, in town, we'll get straight to Watford.

You've had enough crowds and excitement for a convalescent.'

That couldn't have pleased Nicola more. She was beginning to feel very tired. She leaned back and closed her eyes. It would soon be over now. She'd be in her own home, Gran was safely away, and things could get back to normal. She'd allow herself a few days' rest before she began to look for another job.

She started as Saul's hand touched her arm briefly. 'You go to sleep,' he said. 'We shan't be long.'

For the first time she thought she heard real kindness in his voice. Perhaps they could part friends after all.

Saul pushed a cassette into the stereo and the car was flooded with music. This time it was Schubert—the 'Trout' Quintet, which was one of Nicola's particular favourites. She was always grateful that from her father she seemed to have inherited a love of classical music, although not the ability to perform it.

It was very hot inside the car. The sun shone relentlessly through the closed window on to Nicola's face and arm. Saul evidently preferred to hear the music without the background noise of an air-conditioner. A love of music was at least one thing she could admire about him. She rested her head against the soft leather of the seat and let the rippling notes cascade over her like a cool stream.

She was half awake and half asleep and was only dimly aware of the man's strong body beside her, of the movement of his arm as he flicked the gears in and out, and she knew that she was enjoying herself in a strange way. It was luxury to be driven in a car like this one, with the music playing and a feeling of utter confidence in the skill of the driver...

* * *

The music had stopped, the sound of the engine had stopped. Nicola forced her eyes open and saw her own front gate. 'Oh, we're here,' she said rather stupidly. Then, pulling herself together, she added, 'Thank you for bringing me home. And—and thank you for everything. I expect you'll want to get away now.'

He was sitting back looking at her with a half-smile, black eyes glinting under heavy lids. 'Aren't you going to offer me some lunch?'

She felt suddenly confused. 'Well, yes, I—of course— I just thought—you'd be in a hurry, perhaps, to get away.'

'No,' he said. 'I don't want to get away. I want something to eat.'

She led the way up the path and opened the front door. Inside, the house felt empty without Gran. She gestured towards the living-room. 'Would you like to sit down while I see what we've got in the fridge?'

'No,' he said, 'I'd like to come and inspect the fridge too.' He was laughing at her now and she felt even more confused. He seemed to be enjoying some private joke.

In the kitchen, he sat down at the small table with the red and white checked cloth, where she and Gran had breakfast. Nicola peered into the fridge, horribly conscious all the time of his eyes watching her. 'There isn't very much,' she said. 'I must go out shopping this afternoon. I could make a cheese omelette if you'd like that.'

'Very much,' he said gravely.

Her hands weren't quite steady as she tipped the egg mixture into the pan and grated the cheese. It was unnerving to be watched so closely all the time. But at last the omelettes were ready and she put the two plates on the table, with a loaf of bread and a dish of butter.

Saul polished off his omelette with relish while Nicola played with hers.

He looked up from spreading butter liberally on a hunk of bread. 'Not hungry?'

'Not very,' she admitted. She was too conscious of him. He seemed to fill the little kitchen with his disturbing masculine presence. He almost seemed like a threat, and yet in some way it was curiously exciting.

He drank two cups of coffee with the last of Gran's home-made cherry Madeira cake. He certainly had a hearty appetite, Nicola thought as she carried the dirty plates to the sink and turned on the tap.

'Thanks, I enjoyed that,' he said to Nicola's back. She was washing the omelette plates for the third time.

He came across and took the mop out of her hand. 'I'll finish cleaning up here,' he said. 'We'd better be good housekeepers and empty the fridge. It doesn't do to leave fresh food hanging around. Have you got a basket or a box or something to put these in?' He had opened the fridge and was carefully stacking the contents on the worktop. 'We'll take this stuff with us. I'm sure Gran would say waste not, want not.'

Nicola was getting angry now, as well as baffled. How dared he come into her kitchen, eat her food, and now start carting the rest away? She picked up a packet of butter and put it back in the fridge and was reaching for the cheese when he gripped her wrist hard. 'Don't fight me, Nicola,' he said quietly. 'It's a waste of time. You go upstairs and pack some things. You won't need to take much. We'll come back here now and again and keep an eye on the house while it's empty and you can pick up more clothes then, and anything else you want.'

She sank into a chair, staring at him with disbelief. 'What are you talking about? I'm not leaving the house empty. I'm not going anywhere.'

'Of course you are,' he said briskly. 'Didn't Gran explain what we'd arranged? You're coming home with me.'

'I'm certainly not,' she said, sitting down again as if she was demonstrating her refusal to move. 'Gran said,' she spoke slowly and clearly as if she were explaining to a not very bright child, 'that you would look after me while she was away. That was all.'

'Exactly.' He folded his arms, looking down at her. 'Well, I can't look after you here. I've no intention of moving out to Watford. Have some sense, girl.'

She stood up again. She felt she would confront him better if she was standing, although she had to look up a long way to the dark, frowning face. 'But I don't need looking after. I'm twenty-two, twenty-three in December, and I'm perfectly capable of taking care of myself. Gran doesn't always realise that. She's brought me up since I was a baby; sometimes she still thinks I'm two years old. But really, your part is over now, Mr Jarrett.' She anchored herself against the sink as she searched for words to convince him. 'When Paul asked me to marry him I told Gran I had just got engaged and that Paul would look after me while she was away, and—that was what I expected to happen,' she added. She bit her lip. This was getting so complicated.

Saul's mouth hardened. 'Still carrying a torch for Paul? My dear girl, Paul isn't capable of looking after anyone—except Paul—and he does that very well indeed.' His mouth drew down at the corners in contempt.

She turned her head away. 'I don't want to talk about him.' She might as well let him think she was yearning for Paul; it would simplify things.

After a moment she looked back at him. 'That was all I meant to do, that night in your car. I simply meant to ask you if you would pretend to be my fiancé, just for an hour or two. It was dishonest, I know, but I did so want Gran not to be disappointed. She's been looking forward for weeks to this trip, and seeing her new great-grandchildren and everything, and I knew she wouldn't go if she thought I was going to be alone here, in any danger. Well, you know what happened. It's all over now and Gran has left and your part is finished. Please don't think you need bother any more about me.'

'Very prettily said.' The black eyes mocked her. 'Now go and pack your things.'

She stood her ground. 'I'm not coming with you.'

He'd started to empty the fridge again and now he swung round. 'Oh, yes, you are, and you're coming as my fiancée. That's a fair exchange, you must admit. I helped you with your "engagement" and now you can help me.'

So he'd got some scheme, had he, and he was going to use her? Probably something much less altruistic than her scheme. 'Help you with what?' she said suspiciously.

'It's a long story; we won't go into it now. But that's how it's going to be. Right?'

He was clever. She had a horrid feeling that he was going to get his own way. But she tried once more. 'And if I won't come with you?'

'Then I'll ring up the number in Melbourne that Gran gave me and leave a message for her, that you've changed your mind and decided to stay here alone. Unless I'm very much mistaken Gran will be on the next plane back.' He gave her an odiously smug smile.

Her heart sank. She knew that was true. 'B-but that's blackmail,' she stammered.

He brushed that aside. 'Oh, by the way,' he said, 'I got this for you in Paris.' He pulled a small case out of an inside pocket and took out a ring—a huge cluster of

diamonds on a slim gold band. 'I think it should fit.'
The diamonds glittered and seemed to dance in the
afternoon sun through the window.

He reached for her hand but she drew away. 'This is
taking things much too far,' she burst out. 'I
won't——'

Ignoring her protests, he took her hand and pushed
the ring on to her third finger. Then, unbelievably, he
smiled at her, still holding her hand. 'It looks very pretty,'
he said. 'It isn't real, of course, any more than our engagement is. But the imitations are so good these days
that I doubt if anyone will notice the difference. Shall
we seal the bargain in the customary way?' He reached
out and drew her close to him. She felt weak with shock
and bewilderment. She put her hand on his chest and
tried to push him away, but his body was hard as a rock.

'This is absurd,' she pleaded. 'Don't...'

But inexorably his mouth came down on hers, his lips
soft and caressing.

At first it seemed as if that would be all. Then she
heard him mutter roughly, 'Oh, my God,' and felt herself
drawn closer against him, his mouth demanding, seeking.

Every nerve in her body responded. The blood ran
hotly through her veins. For two years she had lived
behind a barrier of ice but now this man was breaking
the barrier down, melting the ice, making her shake and
tremble helplessly.

Her hands went up to bury themselves in the hair at
the back of his neck. She returned his kisses with a
hunger that shocked her.

Then, too soon, it was over. He broke off and held
her away, looking deeply into her flushed, troubled face.
When he spoke his voice was harsh and unsteady. 'I'm
not sure how far I want to be a substitute for Paul.'

He took her by the shoulders and turned her round so that she had her back to him. Then he gave her a push towards the door. 'Now go and get packed,' he said.

Nicola ran into the hall and stumbled upstairs.

CHAPTER FOUR

NICOLA sat on the edge of the bed breathing deeply until she had stopped shivering. She had to ignore her shattering reaction to Saul's kiss. It had meant nothing to him but a momentary release of tension, and that was exactly what it must mean to her too. A matter of proximity, to be avoided from now on. He thought she was still in love with Paul so he would surely not want to complicate the situation.

And what *was* the situation? She was caught in a trap, and a trap of her own making. If she didn't do as Saul wanted he would carry out his threat to spoil Gran's holiday; and that mustn't be allowed to happen. So it followed that she had to go along with whatever it was that he wanted of her and presumably she would find that out in due course. She looked down at the fake diamond glittering on her third finger and struggled with a desire to burst into wild laughter. Very appropriate to this ridiculous situation where everything was fake. Reality had disappeared and she was heading for some place—she didn't know where—with a man she knew nothing about, to take part in some mysterious pretence for a reason she couldn't even guess at.

Nicola stood up and began to pack her case. Ah, well, in for a penny, in for a pound, as Gran would say. Only Saul Jarrett wouldn't deal in pennies—or in pounds—more likely in millions. She hoped this pretence wasn't going to involve her in anything dishonest, however mildly. Not even for Gran's sake would she go along with that, she thought as she snapped the lock of the case, tidied her hair and repaired her make-up, and went downstairs to join him.

'I've made the acquaintance of your next-door neighbour,' he told her, 'and explained the position. She was very co-operative and thought I was doing the right thing to take you away while your grandmother was absent. Gran must have broken the glad news of our engagement and the good lady was very complimentary. I think I made a reasonably good impression.'

I bet you did, Nicola said to herself darkly. He could charm any woman if he cared to, even Mrs Sugden, who had a critical eye for other people's shortcomings.

He picked up her bag and carried it out to the car. Nicola closed the front door behind her and followed him out.

As he took the road into London she said, 'Where are we going?'

He kept his eyes straight ahead. 'I'm taking you home, as I told you.' And then he said, with a faint smile, 'Don't worry, little girl, you'll be quite safe there.'

In spite of the sarcasm, Nicola felt relieved. She had been picturing Saul's home as a luxury penthouse flat, and the implications of his taking her to his flat were—— She refused to consider it. Perhaps 'home' meant a country cottage with a nice body as house-keeper. But he had said he wanted her to help him. How could she help him in a country cottage? She looked up at his profile, at the firm chin and dominant nose, at the long, curving lashes and the lock of black hair that fell forward on to his forehead, and guessed that his thoughts were far away from her, and that he was in no mood to reply to questions.

He spoke suddenly and she blinked, hoping he hadn't been aware of her scrutiny. 'Take a look at the tapes in the locker,' he said. 'We need some music.'

That was an order she was pleased to obey. She sorted through the pile of tapes. They were a mixed bag—classical, jazz, western, pop, blues. Saul catered for all tastes in providing entertainment for his—feminine?—passengers. She selected a Beethoven quartet and pushed it into the stereo. As the first bars sounded she watched Saul's face and saw the dark brows lift a fraction. 'What's the matter?' she enquired. 'Isn't it to your taste?'

'It's very much to my taste. I was a little surprised that so mature a work should appeal to one of such tender years.'

He couldn't miss a chance to put her down, could he? 'Oh, be quiet,' she snapped. 'I want to listen.'

He shrugged, grinned, and said no more. But for once the familiar and well-loved music didn't have its usual effect of putting everything else out of Nicola's mind. She was disturbed to have to admit that in an odd way she was looking forward to what lay ahead. At the very least it would be a change from her usual routine and if Saul wanted her to work for him as a secretary that would present no problems. But if so, why was it necessary to pass her off as his fiancée? Nicola felt an odd little surge of excitement as she reflected that she was about to take a step into the dark.

Half an hour later the music was coming to an end and Nicola looked out of the window but she had no idea where they were. They seemed to have avoided the centre of London and were driving now along quiet suburban roads with large houses. The houses became larger and more spaced out as they drove on. Finally they were in the country. She searched for landmarks. There was something vaguely familiar about this place but she couldn't believe she'd been here before. Then the car turned off the road and into a long, gravelled drive with shrubs on either side and suddenly the light dawned. This was Saul's aunt's house, where she had been to the party.

She looked up at Saul. 'But this isn't——' she began, and stopped as she saw the look on his face.

He was cursing violently under his breath. 'Oh, God, I forgot. It's Friday. Aunt Eleanor's bridge afternoon.' He got out and opened the door for Nicola, grasping her hand tightly to lead her into the house. 'Come along—quick—we'll have to disguise ourselves as part of the wallpaper and hope we won't be spotted.' Then he groaned. As they went into the enormous tiled hall, four women were chatting beside the centre table. Elegant sundresses showed off expensive tans, white hair was discreetly blue-rinsed, perfumes threatened to eclipse that of the bowl of rosebuds on the table.

One of the women detached herself from the group when she saw Saul and ran over to him. 'Saul—what a lovely surprise; we haven't set eyes on you for weeks,' she gushed, and was joined a moment later by the other three.

After effusive greetings were over all four of them cast enquiring glances towards Nicola, who stood there, rather enjoying Saul's discomfiture, and waiting to see what he would say.

Saul might be annoyed but he didn't lose his cool. Solemnly, one by one, he introduced Nicola to the ladies, whose names she promptly forgot, as 'Nicola Oldfield, my brand-new fiancée'. Little well-bred screams of surprise and delight greeted his announcement and Nicola found herself retreating into an acceptable cloak of blushes and shy glances.

A high, light voice sounded from an open doorway. She remembered that voice only too well—Paul's mother.

'Table up,' she cried. 'Back you go, all of you.'

She started to shepherd the four women into the large room where Nicola could see women sitting at tables laid out for bridge, and was turning to follow, when she caught sight of Saul, with one arm round Nicola, making for a passage at the side of the hall. 'Hello, Saul,' Mrs Jarrett called brightly. 'How was Paris?'

She looked at the girl by his side without interest. She was no doubt accustomed to seeing Saul's girlfriends turning up here. Then she looked again and stopped dead, staring as if she couldn't believe her eyes.

'Saul,' she said sharply, and he had to wait while she walked across the hall and stood before them. Saul's arm was still round Nicola, one hand locked on her forearm to display the glittering diamonds on her finger.

Mrs Jarrett stared at it as if she had seen a poisonous snake with its fangs bared. Nicola could see the confusion that was passing through her mind. Her poise slipped, her mouth fell open. 'Why, it's—it's——' she said in a strangled voice.

Saul's poise had *not* slipped, not a fraction. 'It's Nicola Oldfield, Aunt Eleanor.' He smiled broadly. 'I think you two may have met before. Nicola has just done me the honour of promising to be my wife.'

Eleanor Jarrett stared from one to the other of them. She had gone very pale. 'But I don't understand—I thought Paul——'

Saul put a hand on her arm and said soothingly, 'Don't upset yourself, Eleanor. You go back to your bridge ladies; they'll be waiting for you. We'll see you at dinner when all will be explained.'

He shooed her across the hall playfully and when she had gone he turned back to Nicola, taking his arm from her waist. 'This way,' he said, and strode ahead along a passage leading off the hall. There was a door at the end, which he opened with a key. 'My front door,' he said over his shoulder. 'I keep it locked. It gives me a feeling of privacy, which is essential to me.'

Inside the door was a square hall with doors leading off. Saul stood still and shouted, 'Tubb!'

A small, stocky man, neatly dressed in dark trousers and a striped shirt, appeared immediately, and Saul greeted him with an easy smile. 'Nicola, meet Tubb, who looks after me here. There's very little Tubb can't do; he can even produce a cordon bleu meal at a pinch. Tubb, this is Miss Oldfield, my fiancée.'

Tubb's bright little eyes widened. 'That *is* good news, sir. May I congratulate you both?' He shook hands with Nicola and then with Saul. Nicola thought he looked quite amazed. She guessed that Saul didn't make a habit of introducing a future wife, among what was surely an assortment of girlfriends.

'Can I get you anything for a celebration sir?' Tubb suggested.

Saul glanced at his watch. 'We'll postpone the celebration, I think. If you could produce some tea it would be most welcome, eh, Nicola?'

Nicola agreed fervently and Tubb hurried away, while Saul led her into a long room with a window overlooking the garden. Nicola looked round her in surprise. She would have expected Saul's living-room to be furnished in a modern-executive style, but the only modern thing she could see in it was an impressive hi-fi system standing in a recess. The patterned carpet was faded, the brown velvet chairs and sofa well-worn but comfortable-looking. There was an oak dresser with cupboards and drawers and a small dining-table with two chairs. At the far end of the room a French window led out to what looked like a veranda. At the opposite end was an ornate marble fireplace with a jug of summer flowers standing in the hearth, put there, she guessed, by Tubb. Or—the mind boggled—was there a woman in residence, to whom Saul would have to explain the engagement charade he was playing for some unknown reason?

Saul had slumped into a corner of the sofa and thrust out his long legs. 'Nicola, for God's sake come and sit down; you look like a lost kitten standing there.'

She sat in one of the velvet chairs and a spring made a protesting 'ping' and dug itself uncomfortably into Nicola's person.

Saul laughed unkindly. 'Bad luck—wrong chair. Come and sit here instead. I can vouch for the sofa.' He patted the place beside him.

Even to save her pride Nicola drew the line at physical discomfort. She got up and seated herself on the sofa, at the opposite end to Saul.

'Sorry about that,' he said. 'I must have it put right some day.' He sounded weary and Nicola saw suddenly how very tired he was. The dark, handsome face had a drawn look round the nose and mouth and there were black smudges under his eyes. His thick dark hair fell untidily across his forehead. She wondered how he had spent the days in Paris. Was his weariness the result of business pressure—or a round of late-night frivolity? For an unknown reason she found herself hoping it was the former. Then she could feel grateful to him for hurrying back to keep his promise to Gran.

Tubb appeared with the tea. He pulled a small table up to the sofa and set the tray upon it, his bright little eyes resting on Nicola. A fiancée must be something quite new to him, she thought with amusement. Was he fearing he would be supplanted by a mistress in the establishment? she wondered, and wanted to reassure him that the marriage would *not* take place.

'Thanks, Tubb,' Saul said. 'Will you please take a look at the spare room and see that it's in order for Miss Oldfield? Oh, and bring up her case from my car.'

'Very good, sir.' Tubb withdrew.

Saul pulled himself up and pushed the pot to Nicola to pour the tea. 'Tubb's invaluable,' he said. 'Ex-naval. He'll see you have everything you want while you're here.'

Nicola needed to get a few things straight. 'This is your private apartment, I take it. Am I supposed to stay here with you?'

'Why not? You're my fiancée, for the moment. Good grief, don't look like a Victorian parlourmaid being seduced by the wicked squire. I haven't any dark designs on your chastity, I promise you.'

'I think you're being offensive,' Nicola said, slopping tea into his saucer on purpose before she pushed the cup over to him. 'Offensive and—and crude.'

He poured the tea back into the cup and took a long drink. Then he smiled at her wryly. 'You tend to bring out the worst in me, Miss Oldfield. You think I'm a bastard so I tend to act like one.'

She wasn't going to waste time denying that. She drank her tea and ate a biscuit, then glanced at Saul, who was scowling into his cup. It didn't seem a very good moment to tackle him but she had to do it. She drew in her breath. 'Mr Jarrett, I...'

'Saul,' he corrected, without looking up.

'OK, then, Saul. I've got one or two questions to ask.'

'Must you? There are some letters I have to attend to in the office before dinner.'

'Yes, I must, if you want me to go on with this fake engagement. I'm completely in the dark at present.'

He said with assumed patience, 'I merely want you to act as if you were engaged to me—when we're in public. I'm sure you can imagine yourself in that role.'

'I don't have to imagine,' Nicola said bitterly. 'I know how it feels to be engaged—unfortunately.'

At last she had caught his attention. He looked up. 'When?' he said sharply. 'Are you referring to Paul?'

'Oh, no, it was two years ago. The week before the wedding he decided that he didn't want to be married after all. He couldn't take the responsibility.' She didn't wait for any expression of sympathy for none would be forthcoming. She went on, 'You haven't told me anything really. It's all rather embarrassing, meeting people here, as we did a few minutes ago, living in your aunt's house...'

He held up a hand. 'Let's get this straight. The house isn't my aunt's, it's mine. My great-grandfather built it as a family house and it's entailed to pass down the line to the eldest son. It sounds a bit feudal but that's how it is. When my father died, some years ago, I inherited it. My uncle and aunt had been living here with their family, and it continued like that. But the house belongs to me.'

He didn't sound at all proud of his house and Nicola could understand that. She had thought it a cold, cheerless place on the night of the party, and she didn't suppose that anything had changed since. 'I see,' she said slowly. 'Well, that's one point cleared up. But why won't you solve the mystery of why you need a fiancée?'

He brushed that aside. 'There's no mystery.'

'Then why won't you tell me? I explained to you about Gran—when you allowed me to.'

He shook his head. 'Ah, but that was quite different. The fact is that for some reason I seem to value your good opinion. I know it's not very good at present but

I hope to remedy that in the near future. That's why I won't do any more explaining. You're such an innocent, little Nicola.'

His tone made her fume. 'If it's something dishonest,' she burst out, blue eyes flashing, 'then I won't...'

'It's nothing dishonest, I promise. And that's all I mean to tell you at the moment. Just look at me lovingly now and again, as if we were going to be married.' He actually had the nerve to chuckle. 'That shouldn't be so very difficult, surely?'

'Difficult? It's impossible. I wouldn't marry you if you were...'

'The last man on earth?' He was grinning broadly now. 'I believe that's the accepted cliché.'

For the first time his smile wasn't sarcastic, or mocking, and in spite of herself Nicola felt her own lips stretch into an answering smile.

'We-ll, if it were like that, I suppose I'd have to consider it—for the sake of the human race.'

'You think the human race is worth perpetuating? I sometimes wonder.'

'Ah, but then you're a hopeless cynic. I've found that out about you already.' He opened his mouth to protest but she went on, 'OK, Saul, I'll do my best. I suppose I owe you that. But please tell me how I'm going to pass my time here. I can't just sit around doing nothing.'

'Oh, I'm sure you'll find enough to amuse you. You'll be able to help Eleanor with her parties.' He pulled a wry face. 'Eleanor's a great one for parties. There'll be tennis and swimming in the pool and so on. And you might be able to do a spot of work for me. I have an office here and I've just lost the services of my part-time secretary.'

'Yes, I'll do that with pleasure,' Nicola said eagerly. She wasn't very taken with the idea of Eleanor's parties.

'You said you had some letters to do now. Couldn't I type them for you?'

'Oh, I don't think so. They're to our suppliers in Madrid and they have to be in Spanish. My Spanish isn't all that marvellous but I expect I can manage. My late secretary was fluent in Spanish.' He sighed, evidently lamenting his loss.

'I can cope with Spanish,' Nicola said sturdily.

His dark brows rose. 'Really? I'm impressed. And I suppose you're going to tell me you're a genius with a word processor, aren't you? Why on earth were you wasting your time working for cousin Paul?' He slanted her a nasty look. 'Or shouldn't I ask?'

'That's not funny,' Nicola snapped. 'Do you want my help or don't you?'

Saul was on his feet immediately. 'Come this way,' he said.

In the hall he paused, gesturing with an arm. 'Living-room there, kitchen next door, office across the way, Tubb's quarters at the end of the passage. Two bed-rooms upstairs and bathroom. OK?'

Leading the way into the office, he explained, 'My father built this wing on to the house many years ago. We lived here while the other half of the family occupied the main house. It was always supposed to be a family house, but I imagine my father got tired of communal living, if you know what I mean, and I must say I feel the same way. Now, this is my office. Right?'

Nicola looked around. The window was covered by a Venetian blind and between the slats she could see that it faced on to the end of the gravelled forecourt. Shafts of afternoon sunlight lay across an impressive ma-hogany desk which almost filled one half of the office. On the other side were two wooden filing cabinets, and a smaller desk with a word processor on it. A director's swivel chair stood at the far side of the large desk, a small chair on the other side and a typist's chair at the small desk. The carpet was an unobtrusive beige colour and the framed photographs hanging on the wall appeared to be of country scenes. She would examine them later.

Now she was interested in the word processor and to her relief she found that it was the same model as the one she had been using at business school. If the software was similar she would be able to manage very well, but if it was a different system she might need a little while to get used to it.

Saul sat down behind his desk. 'Shall we get on with it, then?' he said briskly.

Nicola hid a smile. Saul was a different man in the office. This was the real Saul, the chief of the venerable firm of Jarrett and Sons, whose reputation he seemed to hold in such high regard—higher regard than anything else—not the Saul who had got himself mixed up with a grandmother and a mock-engagement to a simple, naïve little girl whom he was blackmailing to carry out his wishes for some mysterious reason of his own.

She took the chair opposite him, notebook and Biro at the ready.

Saul pulled a letter from a pile before him. 'Can you read that and give me the gist of it—quickly?'

The letter presented no problem for Nicola. She had studied business Spanish in preference to colloquial Spanish and she read the letter through and said, 'They are enquiring very politely whether we wish to receive a similar consignment of sherry to the order we gave them last year.'

Saul tapped the end of a gold pencil against his strong white teeth. He said at last, 'Will you compose a letter for me, declining the offer, very politely, of course—

you'll know how to put it—but keeping our options open for the future?'

There were two other letters from different firms, and his replies were similar. As Nicola scribbled down his instructions she found herself wondering if Jarretts were running down their stocks, and why. She knew that Paul had placed an exceptionally large order for sherry on his last trip to Spain. He would probably be equally happy-go-lucky about the orders on his present trip. She was well aware, after working with Paul, that he didn't know the meaning of the word economy. He had a reputation in the company for his knowledge of wines, and if he found one he liked he wouldn't hesitate to stock up on it. Saul had been staring down at the desk and now, as if he read her thoughts, he looked up and said, 'We're considerably over-stocked just now. Paul's enthusiasms are apt to run away with him when he's ordering wine.' The dark eyes held hers quite deliberately as he added, 'As they are with his girlfriends.'

To her horror Nicola felt the blood surge into her cheeks. 'May we forget about Paul, please?'

A faint smile touched the long mouth. 'I'll try if you will,' he said.

He was looking at her rather oddly and she couldn't interpret his smile. But then, she thought, she couldn't understand Saul at all. He was an enigma.

She took her notebook and the letters to the word processor and switched it on. She had to get used to it and she hoped Saul would go away and leave her to it. His presence disturbed her.

Once again he read her thoughts, although not, she hoped, for the right reason. He said, 'I'll leave you to see what you can do. I'd better find Eleanor and do a spot of explaining.'

He was away more than an hour and in that time Nicola had made friends with the word processor, written the three letters and printed them out on the firm's notepaper, which she'd found in a drawer. When Saul returned he came straight over to her and stood behind her chair. She handed him the letters and he examined them carefully, with little grunts which she hoped signified approval. 'Excellent,' he said. 'Quite remarkable.' He looked down at her upturned face, which had flushed with pleasure at his praise. Then he smiled slowly at her and to her dismay she felt the flush deepen and her heart begin to thump so hard that she was afraid he would hear it.

He said softly, 'It seems as if I've got myself a first-class secretary as well as a lovely fiancée.' He bent down and planted a kiss on the top of her head. 'Now, come along with me. I'm afraid you've got to confront Eleanor.'

CHAPTER FIVE

As Saul led the way along the passage and into the main hall Nicola braced herself to meet Mrs Jarrett. She wasn't afraid of the woman, but the memory of that awful evening at the party was still fresh in her mind. It had taken an effort of will not to be overawed by Paul's mother and now, not knowing what sort of a reception she would get, she had to summon up that effort again.

Outside the drawing-room door Saul put his arm around Nicola's shoulder and gave her an encouraging squeeze. Perhaps he saw the hesitation in her face for he lowered his lips close to her ear and murmured, 'Don't worry, she won't bite—or if she does, you bite back.'

She turned her head to look up at him and saw the dark eyes dancing with amusement and it gave her a warm feeling that they were partners engaged in some risky enterprise. Perhaps they were, for all she knew.

Mrs Jarrett was sitting in a high-backed chair engaged in some sort of needlework. Coloured skeins of silk lay spread out side by side on a small table beside her, with a work-basket and a vase of pink rosebuds. As Saul and Nicola entered she put down her needlework, took off her glasses and got to her feet, coming to meet them across the long room. She wore a tailored dress of fine wool, which matched the pale grey of her eyes and the streaks in her dark hair. She was smiling brilliantly as she held out both hands to Nicola.

'My dear, now we can meet properly, away from my chattering bridge friends, and I can congratulate you both, and wish you great happiness.'

She leant forward and touched Nicola's cheek briefly with cool lips. Then she reached up and kissed Saul. 'How lovely that you two children are engaged.' She beamed at them both. 'And what a surprise it was.'

'Children, Eleanor?' Saul queried drily.

His aunt laughed. She had a high, tinkling laugh, which Nicola remembered from the party encounter. 'Why, Saul, dear, to me you're one of the younger generation.'

She took Nicola's hand and drew her towards a brocade-covered sofa. 'Now, come and sit down by me and we can have a nice long talk.'

Saul looked down at them. 'If you'll excuse me, I'll leave you two ladies to get to know each other. I've got one or two phone calls to make.'

His aunt gave him an arch look. 'Oh, we can do without you, can't we, Nicola? But you'll both dine with us tonight?'

'Thank you,' said Saul politely, 'we'll be delighted,' and made his escape.

Nicola watched his retreating back resentfully. Traitor! He might at least have stayed to help her out.

Mrs Jarrett waited until the door had closed behind him and then turned to Nicola. 'First of all, my dear, I must apologise for that ridiculous misunderstanding at the party. I blame my foolish son, Paul, very much for that. He confessed to me afterwards that it was all his fault. You'd both been working late, preparing for his trip to France and then you had a meal together and the silly boy said he'd drunk rather too much wine. You're a very pretty girl and he got carried away and he couldn't remember, next day, exactly what he'd said to you. He's so sensitive and he—well, he turned to me to help him clear the matter up.' The tinkling laugh again. 'That's what mothers are for, isn't it? You will forgive us both, won't you?' She touched Nicola's hand.

'Yes, of course, Mrs Jarrett,' Nicola said politely. 'I quite understand.'

'*What* a nice girl you are! And please call me Eleanor, won't you? It's so much more friendly.'

Nicola couldn't think of anything to say and there was a short silence, before Mrs Jarrett went on gaily, 'And all the time you and Saul were getting yourselves engaged and I knew nothing about it. Dear Saul!' Her voice dropped. She sighed deeply. 'He's had such a chequered love life. I was beginning to think——' Then she brightened. 'But now he's found you he will put all the other girls behind him and be very happy.'

Nicola had been prepared to revise her former opinion of Mrs Jarrett, even to like her, if possible, but she decided now that it was quite impossible. The only thing to do was to play the part of the newly engaged girl for all she was worth. 'Other girls?' she queried, letting her mouth droop a little.

'Oh, dear, I shouldn't have said that.' Mrs Jarrett looked stricken. 'My tongue ran away with me. You mustn't take any notice, Nicola. And in any case you know, my child, men will be men, and you'll be the only one from now on, I'm sure. Now let's forget all about that and make some plans. I'll have a nice room prepared for you, overlooking the garden.'

'Thank you, but that won't be necessary Mrs— Eleanor,' Nicola said. 'Saul has made arrangements to put me up in the spare room of his apartment.'

There was another silence. The atmosphere had become chilly. Mrs Jarrett raised thin eyebrows as she said slowly, 'Oh—oh, I see.' She sighed. 'Well, it isn't for me to advise you, of course, but you're very young. Just so long as you know what you're doing.'

Nicola smiled sweetly. She was starting to enjoy herself now. 'Oh, I think I do,' she said, remembering Saul's advice: 'she won't bite—or if she does, you bite back.'

Of course if she'd been engaged to Saul, if she'd been in love with him she would have been devastated by the woman's innuendoes. It was quite evident that Eleanor was opposed to the engagement and was doing her best to cause a rift between Nicola and Saul. But why? If it had been Paul it would have been understandable. She was the kind of woman who would want to choose her son's wife for him. But Saul was merely a nephew by marriage, so what did she have to gain by breaking up the engagement?

What happened next provided a clue. Having issued her disguised warning, Eleanor began to get very cosy. 'Now, Nicola, you must tell me all about yourself; I want to know everything.'

It didn't take very long to disclose all Nicola intended to disclose: she was twenty-two, nearly twenty-three; she lived with her grandmother, her parents having both been killed in a road accident when she was two years old; she had no brothers or sisters; she had taken a secretarial training and had had three previous jobs. Two had been temporary and the third she had lost when the company closed down. She had been very pleased to get a position with Jarrett and Sons six months ago and had been happy working there. She and Paul had got on together well. She had travelled hardly at all; she played tennis in the summer and belonged to a music club; she loved opera on TV and queued at the Albert Hall when the proms were on. 'And that's all about me,' she finished brightly. 'Not very exciting.'

'But what about the young men?' Mrs Jarrett quizzed. 'A pretty girl like you must have had a great many young men after her.'

Nicola was not going into details of her one disastrous attachment. 'If there have been then I've been too busy to notice,' she replied cheerfully.

The other woman was not to be put off. 'And Saul—how long have you known him?'

'Oh, I've known him ever since I joined the firm. But I was impressed with him from the first moment I saw him,' she added for good measure.

'Yes, I'm sure you were.' The words were innocent enough but Nicola detected an undercurrent of sarcasm.

Then Mrs Jarrett lifted Nicola's left hand and examined the engagement ring. Nicola watched her face closely, wondering if she would spot that it was a fake. If she did she showed no sign, except for a slight compression of her lip that might have been a sneer. 'Very pretty,' she said at last.

Nicola took her hand back. 'Yes, I love it. Saul bought it for me in Paris.'

Mrs Jarrett sighed. 'Dear Saul! He's always so generous—and so extravagant. You must be thrilled. Not many girls can boast of owning a ring like this.'

'Oh, I am,' she said demurely. 'It was a lovely surprise.'

Mrs Jarrett nodded and the cross-examination continued. 'And where do you live with your grandmother?'

'We live out at Watford.'

'Watford!' Mrs Jarrett's aquiline nose twitched as if she had come across a nasty smell. 'I'm sure you're very happy there.'

'Yes, very happy.'

The conversation was flagging painfully and Nicola was vastly relieved when the door opened to admit Saul. He had changed his suit for casual clothes and was wearing light trousers and a cream open-neck shirt. His hair was damp from a shower and he looked much less tired.

'Finished your heart-to-heart?' he enquired brightly. 'I've come to take Nicola away, Eleanor; I want to show her the garden.' He took Nicola's hand and drew her to her feet, encircling her waist and drawing her close to him.

Eleanor smiled sweetly up at them both. 'We've had such a lovely talk. I think you're very lucky, Saul, to have found such a nice girl. And she tells me that she was impressed with you from the moment she first saw you.'

Nicola glanced up under her lashes at Saul's face and saw the amusement in his dark eyes. 'Really?' he drawled. 'I'm too modest to believe that. Sweet of you to say so, my darling.' He bent his head and kissed her full on the lips.

A tingling feeling ran all down her body and she went limp at the knees. She felt a little scared—she was playing with dynamite if she gave in to the potent attraction of the man.

She hardly knew how they got out of the house but a minute or two later they were walking across velvety lawns towards a tall laurel hedge. She tried to move away but he kept his arm firmly round her. 'We can be seen from the drawing-room, and I bet Eleanor's looking out of the window.'

Nicola was still feeling a little dizzy after that kiss. She said, 'Need you be so—so demonstrative?'

He chuckled. 'Oh, I think so. We must make it convincing. And I enjoyed kissing you. Didn't you enjoy it?'

'No, of course not. I don't enjoy kissing strangers.'

He put a finger under her chin and turned her face towards him. 'Am I really a stranger? After all we've been through together? You remember I made an impression on you the first time you saw me.' His tone was gently mocking.

'Yes, you certainly did,' Nicola said witheringly. 'And it was decidedly *not* a favourable one. Quite the reverse, in fact.'

They passed through an archway in the laurel hedge and Nicola pushed his arm away. For a moment, without the warmth of it, she felt lonely. This wouldn't do at all, she told herself, and remarked brightly, 'I like the look of the tennis court.'

'You enjoy tennis?'

'Yes, very much. I belong to a local club.'

'And swimming?'

'I love swimming.' Thank goodness they'd moved away from personal topics.

'There's a pool over there; let's have a swim before dinner.'

Nicola hadn't noticed the weather, but now she realised that the June day had been extremely hot. A swim would be heaven. 'But I haven't brought a swimsuit with me,' she said, disappointed.

'No problem,' he assured her. 'Eleanor thinks of everything.'

The pool, when they reached it through another gap in the hedge, looked deliciously inviting, pale blue and translucent and glittering in the late afternoon sunshine. Nicola couldn't wait to get in. There was a large wooden hut beside it—almost large enough to be a pavilion— inside which was a cabin-trunk. Saul opened the lid to disclose an assortment of bathing gear of all colours and descriptions.

'You should find something to fit you here. Help yourself,' he said. 'Eleanor keeps a supply in case any of her visitors want a swim and have come unprepared.'

Nicola riffled through the pile, rejecting the eye-catching bikinis and choosing a black one-piece swimsuit. 'This should do,' she said, holding it up.

'What, no bikini?' He laughed at her, black eyes dancing. 'I'm disappointed.'

She gave him a mock-reproving glance. 'I go in for serious swimming,' she told him.

'Yes, I should have guessed as much. You're a serious girl, aren't you?'

There was a door at either end of the hut. 'That's yours——' Saul pointed to one '—and this is mine,' pointing to the door at the other end. 'Strictly segregated, you'll notice.'

'That's a relief.' She grinned back at him. It was pleasant to share a joke. It made the situation easier.

She went into her own cubicle and closed the door. It was quite a luxurious affair with padded seat, fleecy green towels and a shelf holding toiletries, with a mirror over it.

She slipped off her clothes and climbed into the swimsuit with a feeling of anticipation. It fitted perfectly. She ran her hands down the slim curves of her body and found herself thinking of that last kiss of Saul's. He was so wildly attractive physically. You just keep out of danger, Nicola Oldfield, she told herself. You're not in his league, as his ghastly aunt is so keen on reminding you. And as she reached for the door-handle she pulled the swimsuit up a couple of inches higher round the neck.

Then she noticed the ring. Better take it off; there might be problems if it started to fall to bits in the water. Grinning at the idea, she slipped the ring off and put it on the shelf among the pots and bottles, where it stood winking and flashing at her in the shaft of sunshine that came through the small high window. Without the ring her hand felt curiously naked. A sudden shiver passed through her as she remembered that it had felt exactly the same when she'd taken Keith's ring off and given it back to him. But this was quite different, of course.

She heard Saul's bare feet come padding out of his cubicle and stood on tiptoe to see him running along the side of the pool to the deep end. Stripped he really did look magnificent, she had to admit. He was lightly tanned all over and the muscles of his back and legs rippled as he ran. He was the shape a man should be—long legs, wide shoulders and hips narrow and taut under his dark red trunks. He looked superbly fit and she wondered how he managed to stay that way, sitting behind a desk most of the day, as he presumably did. Squash? Tennis? Running? It was crazy to be 'engaged' to a man you knew nothing about. She'd better find out something if they were to avoid embarrassing moments.

He was standing waiting as she joined him at the deep end of the pool. He surveyed her slowly from head to feet and back again. 'Very nice indeed,' he murmured.

She felt a wave of heat spread upwards under the narrowed dark gaze. She looked down at the water. 'Race you?' she said. 'Two lengths if you give me a five-second start.'

'Right.' They lined up.

Nicola hadn't swum much since she left school, where she had been in the team, but she hadn't forgotten how to do a racing dive. Soon she was striking out strongly for the far end of the pool, her senses tingling with the excitement of the race. She heard Saul come up behind her but she reached the end first and turned seconds ahead of him. But halfway back he overtook her and was waiting for her when she reached the deep end.

She clung on to the rope, laughing with pleasure. 'Ooh, that was lovely,' she gasped, 'but I'm out of practice.'

'You're good,' Saul said. 'I had to exert myself to catch you.'

She shook her head and her wet hair flapped round her face. 'You're just being kind.'

He reached out and pushed the hair back, cupping her chin and looking deep into her eyes. 'I'm never kind, sweetheart. I'm a monster. Didn't you know?' He bared his teeth and growled.

He looked quite different, his black hair plastered wetly to his well-shaped head, his teeth very white against the tanned skin of his cheeks. Younger, more approachable.

She shook her head, looking up at him through her lashes. 'I don't know anything about my fiancé,' she said demurely.

His hand snaked round her waist. 'We'll soon remedy that,' he said, and pulled her under the water.

She gasped and struggled but for a moment she was drawn tightly against him, body to body, as if they were one person. She felt a wild, primitive exultation before they surfaced again. 'First lesson,' Saul said. For a moment longer he went on holding her and then, abruptly, he turned and swam away from her.

Nicola was breathing fast and Saul had covered several lengths before she regained some sort of composure. When she had got her breath back she paddled about slowly. The energy for swimming seemed to have gone out of her. Her limbs felt weak and shaky. Finally she pulled herself out and sat on the side of the pool, wrapping a towel round her.

Saul was pounding along like a speed-boat, brown arms cleaving the water, head rising and falling rhythmically as he took in air. He swam magnificently. If he'd been another man she might have suspected that he was showing off but Saul Jarrett didn't need to prove anything. His self-confidence was as superb as his swimming prowess.

Eventually he stopped, heaved himself over the edge and sat beside her. She felt suddenly shy. She pulled the towel closer round herself and moved a couple of inches away, trying to think of something to say. Eventually, she managed to smile and, 'Next stop Boulogne?'

He flexed his powerful shoulders. 'Sometimes I fancy I could swim the Channel, but not today. Thirty lengths is my limit. It's a very small pool and I get dizzy after that.'

Another silence fell between them. Nicola watched his feet as they splashed in the water below, his long legs, his knees curled round the edge of the pool-surround, his strong thighs with the smattering of black hair.

It struck her like a thunderbolt—the sudden urgent need to reach out and touch him. It was so overwhelming that for a moment she wondered if she had actually done it. She shivered violently.

Saul said immediately, 'The sun's gone in—you're getting cold. Come along, get some clothes on. We'll go back to the house and you can have a warm shower and rest for a bit before dinner.' He pulled her to her feet.

Nicola's knees felt like elastic. The towel slipped down and he stooped to pick it up. For a moment his dark eyes rested on her body, then he draped the towel closely round her and hurried her to the hut.

She didn't remember much about getting back to the house. There was nobody in the hall and Saul took her through to his apartment and up the stairs.

He opened the door into a large bedroom. 'This is for you,' he said. 'I hope you like it. Shower-room through there, bathroom over the passage. There's only one bath so I'm afraid we'll have to share it. The bathroom, I mean, not the bath.' The dark eyes teased her.

She tried to laugh but her throat wasn't working properly and a hoarse croak was the only result.

He bent his head and peered into her face. 'You look very pale. I do hope you haven't caught a chill.'

'I'm fine,' she said. 'I'll have a shower and then relax for a while. What time's dinner?'

'Around eight,' he said. 'Let's meet downstairs at half-seven, and fortify ourselves with a drink before we go in.' He went out and closed the door.

Nicola sat on the edge of the bed, hugging her arms round her body, letting herself listen, at last, to the voice inside that said, You fool, you're falling in love with him.

'I can't be,' she whispered aloud. 'It's too quick, only a few days, and I don't even like him.'

The voice assured her that time and liking had nothing to do with it, and she knew that was true. She lay back on the bed and for a time let herself bathe in the warm bliss of being in love. She spoke his name over and over and her bones turned to water as she relived that moment in the pool when he had held her close against him.

But the euphoria couldn't last. She had to face the immediate future and she didn't know how she was going to do it. She would want to die if he found out she had fallen for him. And she wouldn't be able to trust herself if he touched her—kissed her—as he was sure to do. She laughed bleakly. That was his way of encouraging her to look as if she was in love with him.

She stood up and began to prowl round the large room. What was she going to do? Perhaps if she managed to keep away from him when they were alone she would be able to stay in control and not melt into his arms if he put a hand on her. That was the best she could hope for.

Meanwhile, there was this dinner to be got through. She groaned as she unpacked her bag and put her clothes away. Then she had a warm shower and washed her hair, drying it with the small drier she had seen on the dressing-table.

She hadn't expected to need a party dress, but she'd brought one with her—just in case. She took it off its hanger now and held it up. She'd had it for two years but dresses like this didn't really date—she hoped. It was pure silk, midnight-blue, and it had seemed horribly expensive when she'd bought it, but she'd splashed out on it because Keith, who was inclined to be romantic, had seen it in a shop window and said it matched her eyes. She hadn't worn it since Keith's departure but now a little smile played round her mouth as she thought of him and knew that the dress no longer had any sentimental feeling attached to it.

She shook the dress out and laid it on the bed while she attended carefully to her make-up and brushed her hair until it shone. She had to look her best tonight. Not, of course, that she expected Saul to fall in love with her. That wasn't going to happen, she was quite sure. She had an idea that he had begun to fancy her, but that wasn't any good either. He would probably fancy any reasonably attractive girl he was with. No, she was dressing to please herself, out of pride. And so that she wouldn't let herself down before Saul's snobbish aunt.

Her watch told her it was half-past seven. She slipped the dress over her head and, standing in front of the tall mirror, she inspected the result. She'd lost some weight in the last two years but the dress still fitted perfectly. It was sleeveless, with a draped neckline, low at the cleavage. The skirt hung in soft pleats to below her knees. The silk shimmered as she moved. Yes, it would do; she didn't think Eleanor could turn her nose up at it.

There was a cut-glass bottle of perfume on the dressing-table. An engaged girl would be supposed to wear perfume, she supposed. She touched the stopper to her wrists and temples lightly. She didn't know what it was but it smelled heavenly.

For a while, as she showered and dressed, she had held the thought of Saul away from her, but now it came back in full force, and her stomach felt hollow as she went slowly downstairs to face him.

He was standing beside the drinks cupboard. He was wearing a faultlessly cut light suit and a Paisley tie. He had shaved and brushed his dark hair carefully. Nicola felt the breath leave her body as she looked at him. He really was fabulous to look at, a man any girl would be thrilled to be seen with. She had to remind herself quickly of all the girls who certainly had been.

'What can I get you to drink?' he said.

She hesitated. 'I suppose we'll be having wine at dinner?'

Saul's mouth turned down. 'If I know Eleanor only the best will do—and plenty of it.' He sounded almost angry and she wondered if he paid all the expenses of the house himself. But surely Saul Jarrett wouldn't notice the cost of a few bottles of wine?

'Then may I have lemonade, please?'

The dark brows quirked. 'Nothing more exciting? Martini? Bacardi? Gin and T?'

She shook her head. 'I don't like spirits, or fancy drinks.'

Saul brought her a tall glass of lemonade with a cube of ice floating in it. 'You are a nice honest girl,' he said. 'Most girls put on a great show of sophistication about drinks, I've found.'

A nice honest girl! How dull that sounded. She took a sip of the lemonade. 'Well, it does taste rather flat. Perhaps I'll have a dash of gin in it after all.'

'That's more like it,' he said and topped up her glass, his dark eyes twinkling under their long lashes.

'Now,' Nicola said, 'will you please tell me who I'm going to meet at dinner? I must try not to make any silly mistakes.'

His eyes moved over her slowly as she stood beside the table in the window. 'If you do make any mistakes I'm sure nobody will notice. They'll all be too busy looking at you. You look enchanting, Nikki.'

She felt a tremor inside at his use of the little pet name. 'Enchanting? Me? Surely not.' She took a long gulp of her drink and wondered if gin steadied the nerves or not.

'Oh, yes, indeed you do.' His voice had dropped to a low note and he looked straight into her eyes for a couple of moments, in a way that made her look away.

He poured himself out another small whisky. 'Let me see, there'll be Eleanor, of course, and Colonel Warwick, a devoted admirer of hers over a great many years. And Toby. I should explain that Toby is Tobias Matthewson, who is retired, and has spent the last five years wondering what to do next.'

'Oh, he must have been the gentleman I met at the party,' Nicola said. 'He was practising his golf and he promised to find Paul for me. That was how I heard that conversation between you and Paul.'

'Ah, I wondered about that. It was surprising to find you there. You didn't look the snooping sort.'

She supposed that might be taken as a compliment but she didn't like the way it sounded. 'Thank you very much,' she said in a chilly voice, turning her back on him to put her glass on the table.

Saul stepped forward and came up behind her, so close that she was trapped between him and the table. 'Don't be angry with me, Nikki,' he said. He was so close that she could smell the clean masculine smell of his skin and feel the warmth of his breath on her neck.

It was like a small electric shock. Her back arched in an involuntary spasm. She was horrified. Had she given herself away? She spun round immediately. 'What was all that about?'

'Just to bring a blush to your cheeks and a sparkle to your eyes. Now, smile at me sweetly before we join the others.'

He was so *complacent*, just playing with emotions. Probably he didn't have any himself, not real emotions. She didn't see how she could go on playing this stupid game because sooner or later he'd find out that she was crazy about him and that would be the bitter end.

Then, like a flash of lightning, she knew what she had to do. It was simple, really.

She smiled brilliantly and, reaching up, rubbed her cheek against his. 'We make a wonderful couple, don't we—darling?' she crooned tenderly. 'Shall we go, then?'

The silk of her dress swished against her legs as she swept out of the door before him.

She didn't see the look of utter astonishment on his face.

CHAPTER SIX

As SAUL opened the door into the drawing-room of the main house Nicola linked her arm with his and rested her head against his shoulder. Her cheeks were still burning and her heart was beating fast. When the eyes of the three people in the room turned towards her she knew she must present a picture of a girl deeply in love. Well, that was what Saul required of her, wasn't it? If he asked her why she'd begun to respond to him so ardently, even when they were alone together, she would say she needed the rehearsal in order to play her part convincingly.

'Ah, here they are,' Eleanor cried. 'Come along in and meet people. What a pretty dress, dear. You look quite charming.' Eleanor herself was wearing an elegant gown of black ring-velvet with pearls at throat and wrist.

Nicola smiled politely, guessing that Eleanor would have been rather pleased if she had turned up in jeans and a T-shirt.

Nicola was introduced to Colonel Warwick, a tall, military-looking gentleman with thinning sandy hair and a clipped moustache. He made a little bow as he took her hand and said all the right things. She almost expected him to click his heels together.

'And you two have met before, I understand,' Saul said as a balding elderly gentleman in a velvet jacket ambled up to them from where he had been standing beside the drinks table. His face was pink and plump and friendly, and Nicola recognised him immediately from the time she had stumbled into the wrong room on the night of the party. 'But in case you haven't been formally introduced,' Saul continued, 'this is Toby, Nicola. Toby is my—uncle by marriage, isn't that right, Toby? And this is Nicola, my fiancée.'

Toby beamed. 'Is it permitted to kiss the bride-to-be, Saul?'

Saul said easily, 'Of course, help yourself,' and Toby kissed Nicola's cheek and, with a sly glance at his daughter, said,

'This young lady saved me from the horrors of your party, Nelly.'

Eleanor did not look amused, and directed the Colonel to open the bottle of champagne, which he hastened to do.

Toby clapped Saul on the back, eyeing Nicola at the same time. 'You're a very lucky man, Saul,' he said.

Saul looked complacent. 'Oh, I am, I am.'

Nicola snuggled up to him. 'And I'm the luckiest girl in the world,' she sighed. If Saul was surprised at the languishing look she gave him he didn't show it.

After that, toasts were duly proposed and drunk and Saul said, 'Thank you all for your good wishes, on behalf of myself and my future wife,' and kissed her briefly. It was all somewhat conventional until Toby began to talk about keeping the family name going and the patter of tiny feet. Nicola guessed that he had been having a few drinks earlier in the evening.

Eleanor said in a voice touched with acid, 'Well, now that the ceremony is over, shall we go in to dinner?'

They all began to troop towards the door, but before they reached it it was pushed open from the outside. A girl stood on the threshold, a vision in gold and white. One look told Nicola that this was Paul's sister, Ros, whose marriage to a Texan millionaire had recently come to an end, and whom she had heard about from Paul but never met.

She was ridiculously like her brother, with small even features and a slightly too large mouth, but Paul's fair good looks were transformed, in his sister, into sheer breathtaking beauty. Her hair was white-gold and hung like a cloud to below her shoulders. Her huge tawny eyes were flecked with gold, her skin tanned to a delicate golden-brown. The cost of her minuscule, startlingly white outfit must have run into four figures. A multiple chain of fine gold hung round her neck and her slim fingers were heavy with rings.

'Hello, everyone,' she said tiredly. 'Hello, Mummy.'

Eleanor flew to embrace her. 'Ros, darling—how lovely! I didn't expect you yet.'

The girl disengaged herself and came further into the room, pulling off her short jacket and flinging it down carelessly. 'It was an impulse. I meant to stay on in New York but it was like a furnace there. I got a cancelled seat on Concorde, so here I am.' She sank into a chair, closing her eyes. 'There's a taxi waiting outside. I only had dollars.'

Eleanor turned to the Colonel. 'Robert—could you?'

'Of course, my dear.' He hurried out of the room.

Ros opened her eyes. 'Is that champagne over there? Pour me a glass, Grandpa, there's a love.'

Eleanor walked fussily to the side-table, took the brimming glass from Toby and carried it back to her daughter, who nodded and took a discreet gulp. 'Ah, that's better.'

'You're tired out, my child,' Eleanor said anxiously. 'Now you stay there and I'll go and see Cook about dinner for you.' She went out of the room, casting a glance at Saul, who hadn't moved since Ros came in.

Now the girl's enormous eyes fastened themselves on him. 'Hi, Cousin Saul. Mummy says you've got yourself engaged. I don't believe it.' She spoke in an intimate drawl.

Saul's tone was even as he said, 'You'd better believe it, Ros. Why don't you drink our health? Nicola—my cousin Ros. Ros—Nicola, my future wife.'

The girl's eyes swept over Nicola briefly. 'How touching! Well, cheers!'

She sipped her champagne and over the rim of her glass her eyes didn't move from his and seemed to hold a challenge. He stood quite still and Nicola thought he stiffened slightly as they went on staring at each other.

The sudden sharp pain that ripped through Nicola was so intense that she thought she might faint, and held Saul's arm tightly. Saul and Ros—this was what it was all about. Ros was free, and Saul wanted her and was playing the old, old game of hard-to-get. When she'd heard of his 'engagement' Ros had hurried home. There was no doubt in Nicola's mind. He had set her up and it was no wonder he had refused to explain. Perhaps he had even felt a tiny bit ashamed of himself, although she doubted it.

Dinner was an uncomfortable meal. Eleanor sat at the head of the table with the Colonel on her right and Saul on her left. This seemed to Nicola rather an odd seating arrangement, as Saul was owner of the house, but it was evidently the usual thing. Nicola sat beside Saul, while Ros was opposite, between the Colonel and Toby, cocooned, as it were, in a tight little family circle, while Nicola, having nothing on her left except the chilly length of empty table, felt herself excluded. No doubt that was what Eleanor had intended.

There was an awkwardness about the conversation— what there was of it. The Colonel devoted himself to Eleanor's needs, while Toby was much too interested in his food and wine to be sociable. Eleanor spent most of the time instructing the little maid who waited at the table and was evidently new to the job in a sign language of beckoning and pointing. Saul didn't say a word.

As dishes of iced melon were placed on the table Ros turned her eyes languidly on Nicola. 'And what do you do?' she asked in a bored tone.

Saul answered for her. 'Nicola used to be Paul's secretary,' he said, 'until I rescued her.'

Ros raised perfect eyebrows. 'How romantic! Quite the Sir Galahad of Jarrett and Sons!' she drawled. 'And the fair damsel is duly grateful, of course?' She swivelled her eyes towards Nicola.

Nicola fought back a temptation to throw her slice of melon into the girl's face. 'I'm very happy, thank you,' she said quietly.

She felt Saul's hand touch her knee under the table. The gesture seemed to say, You're doing fine; keep it up. She moved her leg, turning away.

The melon was followed by roast duck. It was probably delicious but Nicola hardly tasted it. She noticed nothing of the snippets of conversation that drifted into her ears and out again. When the plates were removed and the wine glasses refilled Ros sat back in her chair and sighed. 'It's good to be back again in the shabby old place.'

The word caught Nicola's attention. Shabby? She looked round the luxuriously appointed dining-room with its crimson pile carpet and its richly brocaded curtains in stiff silk. But, of course, Ros had been married to a millionaire, she reminded herself. She'd probably got accustomed to a background like a Hollywood film set.

Eleanor pulled a wry face. 'You're quite right, dear. This room especially needs redecorating. I'll have to see about having it done.'

Saul roused himself. 'Steady on, Eleanor. I expect Nicola will want to make a lot of changes when we're married, and your taste may not appeal to her.'

Eleanor's mouth thinned and the pale grey eyes became icy.

The entrance of the maid with a creamy pudding was a diversion and by the time she had left the room Eleanor had had time to pull herself together. She smiled sweetly. 'Of course, Saul. I keep forgetting, I shall become the dowager then, and be relegated to the dower-house. What a pity there isn't a dower-house to be relegated to.' She gave a brittle laugh.

'Oh, I don't know,' Saul said smoothly. 'I had an idea you might like to change round and take over my quarters, then you could redecorate to your heart's content.'

Now there was no disguising Eleanor's anger, or that she had taken Saul's suggestion as an affront. A dull crimson rose into her cheeks and her fingers drummed nervously on the table. The Colonel put his hand over hers and directed a reproving look at Saul, who went on eating his pudding as if nothing had happened. Ros leaned her elbows on the table, taking in everything, amusement in her gold-flecked eyes. If she felt she should take her mother's part in all this she was making no effort to do so.

Nicola had kept her eyes fixed on her plate through this unpleasant little exchange and now she glanced up at Saul, saying in a low voice, 'Do you think anyone would mind if I went to my room? I've got rather a bad headache.'

'Of course,' he said immediately, pushing back his chair to help her up, and saying to the company in general, 'I don't think Nicola has quite recovered from a nasty fall she had a little while ago.' He put his arm around her. 'Come along, darling, I'll take you up.'

Ros directed a sultry look at him. 'Do come back and have coffee with us, Saul. I've got such a lot to tell you.'

'I might,' he said enigmatically, and led Nicola out of the room.

At her bedroom door she paused. 'Thanks, I'll be fine now.'

He ignored the dismissal. He reached round her and opened the door, following her inside and closing it after him.

'Is your headache really bad?' he said. 'Have you got some tablets for it?'

She walked across to the dressing-table, turning her back on him. 'I haven't got a headache,' she said. 'I didn't want to stay down there being *used* by you, that's all.'

'Used? What the hell are you talking about?'

She said coldly, 'I mean that you were using me and our fake engagement to humiliate Eleanor. You were beastly to her and she was horribly upset.'

He laughed shortly. 'Oh, don't waste your pity on my aunt. Under that elegant exterior she's pure pressed steel.' He came across and put a hand on her shoulder. 'You mustn't be so sensitive, little girl,' he said. 'It'll get you nowhere in this life.'

She spun round to face him. 'The only place I want to get to at the moment is out of this house,' she said. 'I think you're disgusting.'

'Oh, dear!' He pulled down his mouth comically. 'And I really thought you were beginning to like me.'

'Like you? How wrong can you be? I was merely rehearsing my part. I find it very difficult acting as though I'm in love with you. I've needed all the practice I can get. It hasn't been easy. But anyway, there's no need now to go on with this stupid game, is there?'

'No need?' he said blankly. 'Whatever gave you that idea? There's every possible need.' He put a finger under her chin and raised her face to his. 'You promised, Nicola. You're not going to let me down now, just when things are beginning to go well, are you?'

She bit her lip, not meeting his eyes.

'That's my girl. Now you have a good night's sleep. It's been a long day for you. I'll send Tubb in with coffee and biscuits and if there's anything else you would like just tell him. Goodnight, Nikki.' He went out of the room.

Nicola picked up her hairbrush and began to brush her hair violently. Saul hadn't changed. He'd merely been using his charm on her because he wanted something from her. Underneath he was still the arrogant, cynical brute she had first thought him.

How could she ever have imagined she was in love with him? It was simply a kind of teenage crush because he was so stunningly sexy. It wouldn't last long once she was away from this place. Once Saul was sure of Ros the 'engagement' would be at an end, and then she could think about what she was going to do next.

A few minutes later Tubb appeared with a pot of coffee, a plate of biscuits and a bottle of pain-killers. 'There are the ones Mr Saul always uses,' he told her. 'He swears by them. Do ring me if you want anything else, miss.' He grinned his wide grin and departed.

Nicola took off her blue dress and hung it up. Then she got into a dressing-gown and sat down in front of the TV to drink her coffee and watch the ten o'clock news. After that there was a long documentary about South America, then the late film, which was a French classic. She tried to concentrate on it, to use the dialogue to polish up her French, but she found her mind slipping away and knew that subconsciously she'd been listening for Saul to come up and go into his room next door.

She saw the film through to the end. By that time it was after two o'clock and she was shivering with cold and nervous tension. Saul wasn't coming to bed now. He was in another bed, in another part of the house.

Once again jealousy knifed sharply through Nicola as she pictured them together, limbs entwined, mouth locked to mouth. She pulled the dressing-gown tight around her and crept into bed, taking two of the pain-killers Tubb had brought because now she really did have a splitting headache. They must have been very strong indeed, for within ten minutes she was fast asleep.

It was bright daylight when Nicola awoke next morning. She dimly remembered Tubb coming in with a cup of tea, which sat on the bedside table now, stone-cold.

Hastily, without thinking about last night, she got herself up, showered and dressed in jeans and a pullover, and went downstairs.

Tubb was Hoovering the hall carpet. He switched off the machine when he saw her. 'I hope you're feeling better, miss. Mr Saul has had his breakfast. Shall I bring toast and coffee for you, or would you like something cooked?'

'Oh, just toast and coffee, please,' Nicola said hastily, returning the man's smile. Her cheeks felt stiff with the effort.

The table in the living-room was set for one. Nicola was finishing her second cup of coffee when Saul walked in. His hair was wet and he had a towel draped round his neck. He was naked from the waist up, and Nicola's stomach churned as she looked at him.

He stood just inside the door. 'Good morning, Nikki,' he said. 'Are you feeling better? I've just been for a quick dip.' His voice was absent and she noticed lines of tiredness under his eyes. No wonder, she thought bleakly.

'I'm sorry I'm late down,' she said. 'Did you want me to start work in the office?'

'When you're ready. I'll go up and put some clothes on and join you there in ten minutes.' He departed up the stairs.

Nicola heard the phone buzzing on her way to the office. After waiting for a moment to see if Saul would answer it in his room, she picked up the receiver. 'Mr Jarrett's office.'

A voice checked the number, then, 'Your call to Melbourne,' it said.

Nicola collapsed into a chair. 'Hello,' she gasped. 'Who is that?'

'Nicola—this is Gran.' The voice was shaking with excitement. 'I can't believe it—that I'm in Australia and talking to you in England.'

It took a few moments to get over their mutual amazement, but soon Gran was in high spirits as Nicola fired questions at her. Gran said the babies were adorable and the family were all darlings and delighted to see her. She was going to be driven out to their new ranch and they all sent their love and said Nicola and Saul must come and visit them when they moved.

Then it was Gran's turn to ask questions and Nicola managed somehow to produce the replies that would assure her that all was well.

'And Saul?'

'Oh, Saul's wonderful.' She was proud of the warmth in her voice—the kind of dreamy warmth that Gran would expect. 'He's not here at the moment but he sends his love. I'm staying with his aunt just now and the house is beautiful.' She went on to talk glowingly about the garden, the tennis court and the swimming-pool. 'I'm going to swim every day. It's just like being on holiday. Give my love to everybody, and I'll write to you very soon.'

She put down the receiver and turned to see Saul standing in the doorway wearing grey trousers and a grey silk shirt.

'I'm so glad you think I'm wonderful. You certainly sounded as if you meant it.' He came over to where she stood beside the desk. His tone was half teasing, half questioning. When she didn't make any reply he went on, 'I booked the call through half an hour ago. I thought it would be a nice surprise for you when you woke up.'

He had wanted to please her. She would have liked to throw her arms round his neck and thank him. But last night had shown her what his motives were in handing out a sweetener to her now and again.

'It was a nice surprise,' she said composedly. 'I'm very grateful. Gran sounded delighted with everything and she enjoyed the flight.'

At that moment the phone rang again and she reached out for it.

'OK,' said Saul. 'It's only the fax.'

The machine on the desk fed out three sheets. Saul picked them up and leafed through them quickly. 'Damnation!' he muttered. 'I thought I'd got it cracked but this means I'll have to go up to the London office straight away. Sorry, Nikki; I'd hoped we might have a game of tennis but I'm afraid it's off for today. I'll get back as soon as I can. Look after yourself.' He was frowning as he touched her shoulder absently and she saw that he had already forgotten all about her.

He picked up the briefcase, stuffed the fax sheets inside and strode out of the room. A moment later she heard the front door slam.

Without Saul the house was empty and dead. Nicola spent an hour concocting a long letter to Gran. It was the first time she'd deceived her; their relationship had always been open and she'd thought of Gran as a friend and confidante. Gran had always kept herself up to date with current attitudes and never made judgements of any kind, moral or otherwise. Nicola asked herself how she was ever going to explain the whole truth to her in the end. The more she thought about it, the more difficult it seemed to be and in the end she gave it up and went looking for Tubb, to ask for a long, cool drink, for it was getting very hot.

He brought her a tall glass of orange juice with a cube of ice floating in it, and suggested that she might like to sit out on the side-veranda. 'It's private to Mr Saul,' he said, 'and it'll be nice and cool for you. It's going to be a sizzler later on.'

That suited Nicola very well. She didn't want to encounter any of the family when she was alone. She pulled a book at random from the bookcase and followed Tubb through the French window on to the veranda, where he placed a chair beside a white garden table and assured himself of her comfort.

As Saul had said, Tubb was certainly a gem. Nicola asked him about his days in the Navy and listened with interest to his talk of some of the action he had seen around the world. He would probably have gone on for hours if he hadn't suddenly remembered that he had been jointing a chicken in the kitchen and was afraid 'that darned Bo'sun will have his nose into it'.

'Bo'sun? Who's he?' Nicola enquired, and Tubb told her that Bo'sun was a tabby cat who'd walked in one night 'as thin as a rake and bleeding from one ear'. Tubb had cleaned him up and fed him and he'd been here ever since.

'He's a nice old fellow but he's got a sort of liking for chicken,' Tubb added as he hurried away.

Nicola thought his fears were groundless, as a large tabby cat—most probably the cat in question—strolled in from the garden almost as soon as Tubb departed. Having decided to approve of her, he jumped up on to her knee, kneaded his paws on her jeans and made himself comfortable there.

Nicola's spirits revived. She seemed to have made two friends in this house. She settled down to read her book, stroking the furry head while Bo'sun purred lazily. Sunshine filtered warmly between the vines trailing over the wooden slats which formed a canopy overhead. Bees buzzed. Butterflies invaded a buddleia bush. Nicola closed her eyes.

Suddenly she opened them again, aware that somebody was there.

Ros was standing a couple of yards away, staring at her. She wore a scarlet sundress and her white-gold hair was piled on top of her head. A scarlet beach-bag was hitched carelessly over her shoulder. She looked very beautiful and very sulky.

'Where's Saul?' she demanded.

Nicola looked her up and down slowly. She had met women like this before, who believed that rudeness was a sign of blasé sophistication. 'Saul's gone to London,' she replied quietly.

Ros flopped into a chair. 'Oh, damn, I wanted to talk to him.' She sat looking sulkily down at her white kid sandals.

Nicola studied the girl's face quite deliberately. Ros was older than she had thought last night—nearer thirty then twenty, she judged, as she noticed the tiny lines round her mouth and eyes.

Ros must have become aware of Nicola's scrutiny for she sat up and rummaged in her beach-bag for a pair of enormous sunglasses, which half covered her face.

Nicola's own sunglasses lay on the table beside her. She reached for them, and as she adjusted them she thought with black humour that she and Ros were like a couple of fencers pulling down their visors before a contest.

Ros had evidently been planning her line of attack. She said abruptly, 'You know why Saul got engaged to you, don't you?'

This was going to be tricky. It would be amusing to try to hold her own without telling lies. 'Of course I know,' Nicola said coolly. 'Because he wanted to.'

This was evidently not the reply Ros had expected. 'You don't imagine he's going to marry you, do you?'

'Oh, I don't have to imagine anything. I know.' That was true, unfortunately.

The great sunglasses were turned full on her. 'You're very pleased with yourself, aren't you?' Ros was beginning to show signs of being slightly ruffled. 'He won't marry you, you know. Not now I'm free. Saul and I have always been meant for each other. We fell in love in our prams. I made a silly mistake when I was very young and foolish, but I'm free again now. I couldn't decide whether to come home and I suppose he calculated that if he got himself involved with some cheap little typist that nobody knew it would make me jealous and I'd come back to him. It's the oldest trick in the world. Well, it worked, and here I am. So don't you think, my dear, that it's time you removed yourself from the scene?'

Nicola was cold with rage. She put Bo'sun off her knee and stood up. 'I think it's time *you* removed yourself,' she said icily. 'This is Saul's private apartment, and you're not welcome here.'

Ros was on her feet too. She was several inches smaller than Nicola. 'Who the hell do you think you are?' Her voice was shrill. 'You can't order me about like that.'

Nicola took a step forward, feeling herself in command now. 'Oh, indeed I can,' she said in a low, steely voice. 'Now get out.'

Ros stumbled down the steps of the veranda. 'You'll be sorry for this,' she blustered as she flounced away round the corner.

Nicola had never felt angrier in her life. The violence of her emotion frightened her. She was shaking all over and she felt as if she was going to choke. How dared Saul go off and leave her undefended against that abominable woman? It was intolerable of him. The whole situation was intolerable and she wasn't going to endure it any longer. Why should she? He'd got what he wanted, she thought bitterly, what he'd used her for. He'd got Ros into his bed last night.

Nicola tasted blood as her teeth dug into her lower lip. She felt humiliated, degraded. She'd be justified in leaving straight away, this moment, but that would be cowardly. She'd wait until he came home. She beat her fist on the back of the chair. If only he were here now and she could tell him exactly what she thought of him! But he wasn't here and wouldn't be back for hours and she had to fill in those hours somehow. She needed action, something physical. Walking would tire her body and clear her mind, ready to confront him. She set off round the corner of the house and down the drive at a fast pace.

At first she encountered nobody but when she reached the entrance gates a car came up behind her and she drew aside to let it pass. It was the grey Rolls-Royce which had met her at the station on the night of the party. The uniformed chauffeur was at the wheel and behind him, sitting upright and looking straight ahead, sat Ros, her scarlet dress a danger signal, her hair gleaming silver in the sunlight. Ros was on her way to London after Saul, of course.

Impotent rage gripped Nicola as for the first time in her life she knew what it was like to feel murderous.

As the Rolls passed between the gates the chauffeur touched his cap in a courtesy salute. Ros didn't move her head. The car turned left and swept away in the direction of the station.

Gritting her teeth, Nicola strode off down the lane in the opposite direction.

CHAPTER SEVEN

Two hours later Nicola, dusty, sticky and exhausted, limped across the veranda and into the living-room, where Tubb was hovering.

'Ah, there you are, miss. I came to tell you lunch was ready but you'd disappeared.' His keen little eyes surveyed her with a worried frown. 'Are you all right, miss?'

She made a wry grimace. 'I've been for a walk,' she told him.

He looked shocked. 'Oh, you didn't ought to have gone walking in this heat, miss. You've tired yourself out.'

'I think you may be right, Tubb,' Nicola admitted, pushing back a damp lock of hair and easing her T-shirt away from her neck. 'I'll go and get tidy before lunch.' She looked round cautiously. 'Has Mr Saul come home yet?'

Tubb shook his head. 'No, miss, he hasn't.'

That was a relief, she thought as she climbed wearily upstairs. She wouldn't have cared to face Saul looking a wreck.

The walk had been a nightmare. As soon as the lane joined the main road there was no shade against the blistering heat of the sun, and a continuous stream of traffic thundered past in both directions. There seemed to be nowhere else to walk and Nicola had trudged on doggedly, determined not to go back until she'd worked off the fury that still boiled inside her. She didn't know how far she'd walked—a mile, two miles, three?—before she'd turned and retraced her steps, her head aching, her feet hurting, and her throat full of traffic fumes. But at least, she thought, as she stepped under a cool shower, the walk had served its purpose. The boiling anger had simmered down into indignation at Saul's contemptible behaviour. She could face him now without the fear of bursting into hysterical accusations against him, against Ros, against Eleanor, against the whole miserable setup.

Half an hour later she returned to the living-room, looking cool and groomed in a white seersucker dress patterned with dark blue cornflowers.

Tubb had set a cold lunch at the table in the window and she persuaded herself that she was hungry. But when, half an hour later, Tubb came in to clear the dishes her plate was pushed aside, the salad only half eaten, and Nicola was sitting staring blankly out of the window, her elbows on the table, her chin cupped in her hands.

She started when she saw him. 'Sorry, I was miles away.' In her mind she'd been in London, where Saul and Ros were gazing into each other's eyes over a restaurant table. 'The salad was lovely. I'm afraid I haven't got much of an appetite.'

'You've tired yourself out, miss, going walking in that heat! It's been something dreadful—there's going to be a storm before the night's out, you'll see.'

He lingered, holding the loaded tray in front of his stocky body. 'Er—do you happen to know what time Mr Saul will be home, miss?' When Nicola shook her head, he went on, 'You see, it's like this. Saturday's my evening off and Mr Saul usually eats out, but he didn't say anything this morning and I thought, as you were here, miss, that I'd have something cooked, just in case. There's a chicken casserole in the oven, doing very slow, and I was wondering if you would...'

Nicola held up a hand. 'Say no more, Tubb. Just show me where things are before you go, and I'll feed Mr Saul when he comes in.'

Tubb looked relieved. 'You see,' he confided, 'I'm in the final of the darts competition down at the pub and I wanted to be away in good time. Half-five, if that's OK with you.'

Reassured on that point, he departed. But he had hardly had time to carry his tray to the kitchen when a buzzer sounded and he hurried to the front door.

Nicola groaned as she heard voices in the hall. Eleanor! To be sniped at by Eleanor after Ros's attack would be too much to bear.

The door opened a crack and Eleanor's immaculate head appeared round it. 'Am I intruding?' she enquired coyly. 'Saul not home yet?'

Nicola got to her feet and said, with as much politeness as she could muster, 'No, not yet.'

Eleanor, wearing an ivory silk trouser suit, came further into the room. 'Oh, silly me, of course not. Ros went into London to meet him.'

Nicola said nothing. There was a horrid satisfaction about having one's worst fears confirmed.

Eleanor slid her a glance. 'You mustn't mind, dear. Those two are such old friends and they're thrilled to be together again. They've always been very close. There was a time when——' She broke off, sighing.

Nicola would have liked to throw something at that smiling, insincere face. Instead she said politely, 'Won't you sit down?' indicating the chair with the broken spring.

'Thank you, dear, but no, I mustn't stay. I have Colonel Warwick here for dinner—he's playing chess with my father just now—and I must organise the kitchen. You wouldn't care to join us?' she added.

Nicola smiled sweetly. 'No, thank you; I'm expecting Saul in any moment.'

The lift of Eleanor's eyebrows expressed her disbelief. 'Of course,' she murmured.

There was a short silence before she went on, 'What I came about was to tell you that I'm giving a little drinks party tomorrow evening and I hope you and Saul will come along. I'd like you to meet some of our near neighbours; I've told them all about you and they're dying to meet you.'

Nicola would have liked to know exactly what she had told them, but she could guess.

'And I've been very lucky,' Eleanor went on, 'to persuade our local celebrity to come along. I don't suppose you'll have heard of him—like most young people I expect you prefer pop music.' She smiled indulgently. 'He's Sir Victor Wells, the famous conductor.'

Heard of him! Nicola had queued for hours to hear Sir Victor conduct *The Dream of Gerontius* last summer at the Albert Hall.

'I'll have to introduce you,' Eleanor went on, 'but I'm afraid you'll find him rather heavy going. He's a highly—er—cultivated man. I must admit that sometimes I get a little lost myself when he talks about music.' Again the tinkling laugh. 'I promise to come and rescue you as soon as I can.'

'Thank you,' Nicola said woodenly.

'You'll tell Saul, then—when you see him—that I'll be expecting you both? About half-past six?'

'Yes, I'll tell him.' She wouldn't be there, but Saul might like to drop in—with Ros, of course.

She went with Eleanor to the door. 'Hasn't it been a hot day?' she said conversationally. She might as well be polite to Eleanor. She wouldn't be seeing her again.

'Terrific!' Eleanor fanned herself. 'I'm afraid we're going to have a storm. Will you be frightened if you're here alone?'

If Saul is spending the night in London with Ros, you mean? 'Oh, no,' Nicola said airly. 'I rather enjoy storms.' It was a lie; she was terrified of storms, had been since she was a child. But what was one more lie among so many she'd been telling lately?

When the front door was firmly closed behind Eleanor Nicola went into the office and stood for some time looking at the telephone, debating whether she should put a call through to Australia to tell Gran her plans. But what were her plans? She hadn't gone any further than her determination to leave in the morning. And anyway, it would be the middle of the night in Australia.

Back in the living-room she stood staring moodily out of the window. The sun had gone in long ago and dark clouds, like dirty cotton wool, were massing above the trees. Nothing stirred on the terraced lawns. Just a week ago, she thought, she'd walked across these lawns with Paul, among a crowd of guests, to meet Eleanor. Such a lot had happened since then.

She paced about restlessly. Saul and Ros would have finished lunch by now. They had probably gone back to his flat—surely he'd have a flat in town, although he'd never mentioned it. Nicola set her teeth and rehearsed what she was going to say to him when he came in.

The minutes crawled by and the room got darker. Nicola wished the storm would come, if it was going to come, and that applied to the storm down here as well as the one up in the heavens. She was beginning to feel suffocated by the waiting.

Soon after four o'clock Tubb came in with a tray of tea. Nicola thought he looked pityingly at her as she sat curled up in a corner of the sofa, but he merely said in a jocular tone, 'The cup that cheers!' He put down the tray and switched on the table lamp. By now the room was almost dark. 'It's getting quite chilly,' he said. 'The fire's all laid ready to put a match to, miss. There are logs in the basket and matches on the mantelpiece.'

That tea was the nicest thing that had happened all day and she made it last as long as she could, draining the pot and eating two little queen cakes. When the gilt clock on the mantelpiece chimed a quarter-past five she went out to the kitchen and found Tubb polishing a pair of sturdy boots.

The kitchen was largish, fully equipped but with fittings of oak, which made it look homely. A wonderful aroma of chicken and herbs came from the Aga. Tubb showed Nicola round with pride. Everything was spotless and tidy. 'The chicken won't come to harm, however long you leave it in,' he told her, sitting on a stool to pull on his boots. 'And I've left a tin of food out for old Bo'sun. He'll be bound to come in for his dinner.'

She promised to feed Bo'sun. 'And mind you win that darts match,' she told Tubb as he took down an oilskin mac from a hook behind the door.

The cheery little man elevated two thumbs, grinning widely. 'I'll do my darnedest,' he promised, and went out.

When the back door had closed behind him Nicola stood still, looking out at the dark masses of cloud. Now that she was alone in the house she felt a great wave of depression settling over her. She sniffed and blew her nose. No point in feeling sorry for herself.

She heard a small sound at her feet and looked down to see Bo'sun gazing up at her hopefully. She picked him up and rubbed her cheek against his soft fur. But Bo'sun wasn't having any of that; he had other things on his mind. He struggled out of her arms and waited expectantly while she opened the tin of food, weaving himself round her legs, purring happily.

She stood watching him until he had finished every bit and licked the bowl clean. A smile touched her mouth. It was so easy to make a cat happy.

She went back to the living-room, Bo'sun padding after her like a small dog. The room wasn't cold but it was cheerless and dark, and Nicola shivered as she drew the curtains and put a match to the fire. She sat on the hearthrug, watching the wood blaze up. Bo'sun sat beside her, washing himself industriously.

It was Bo'sun who gave the first warning of the impending storm. Suddenly he sat up straight, head thrown back, listening intently. Then, with an anguished yowl, he scuttled away to hide in a far corner of the room. A moment later Nicola heard it herself—a low rumble in the distance. Her first impulse was to run upstairs and bury her head under the bedclothes as she had done when she was a little girl. But she told herself not to be silly. She wasn't a little girl now and there was no need to panic. It was only a summer storm and it would soon be over.

In this she was quite mistaken. Next day the newspapers were to report that Kent had suffered its longest and most severe thunderstorm for ten years and much damage had been reported.

As the first blinding flash of lightning found its way between the chinks in the curtains and lit up the room Nicola made a dive for the sofa and burrowed into a corner, pressing cushions against her ears to blot out the thunder—but not in time to escape the vicious clap which followed almost immediately.

That was only the beginning. It seemed to Nicola, as she winced at each ear-splitting crash, her stomach clenching, every nerve taut, that it would go on forever.

She huddled deeper into her corner as the storm gained in ferocity, sometimes receding for a time, then returning with fresh fury, snarling like an enormous wild beast.

Was it never going to let up? Nicola found herself whimpering with terror. Then there was an almighty crash, seeming to split the roof. She jerked up, holding her breath in the silence that followed. Had the house been struck by lightning? Had a thunderbolt fallen? Then into the silence came the rain—a deluge lashing against the windows. By degrees the thunder died away until it was only a continuous rumble in the far distance. Nicola waited, listening to the rain, praying that the storm had really gone for good. When, at last, Bo'sun came back and jumped up beside her, she was sure that it had. Cats knew about these things.

Nicola felt drained of energy, but she had to check that no damage had been done. She dragged herself upstairs to inspect the rooms beneath the roof. When she found nothing to suggest that the house was on fire, or that a thunderbolt had fallen on it, she threw herself on her bed, trembling, and tried to relax.

For a time she slipped into a half-sleep and when she was fully awake again the trembling had stopped and her mind seemed to be clearer. She sat up and looked at her watch. It was twenty minutes to eight. The storm must have lasted the best part of two hours. Saul would have been home long before this, if he had been coming. No, he and Ros would still be in London and would probably spend the night at his flat.

There was one thought uppermost in Nicola's mind— that she was going to get away from this house at the first possible moment and nothing was going to stop her.

As if she needed to support that resolve in a practical manner, she took her travelling bag from the wardrobe and laid it open on the bed. Then she opened the drawer and began to pack away the clothes she had brought with her.

She was folding a summer dress when she heard a step on the stairs. Every muscle in her body stiffened.

'Nikki—Nikki—where are you?'

She didn't answer and when the door opened she didn't even look round. She finished folding the dress and packing it away.

'What the hell are you doing?' His voice was slurred, as if he'd been drinking.

'Packing,' she said. 'I'm leaving here in the morning.'

'Oh, no.' It was a groan, deep in his throat.

She spun round, keyed up to fight him if necessary, in time to see him stagger and collapse on to the bed. He looked terrible. His face was ashen and his clothes were soaking wet and covered in mud.

Nicola was across the room in a second, all her anger forgotten. 'Saul—Saul—what's happened? Are you hurt? Shall I send for a doctor?'

Oh, God, she thought, a car smash. He was badly injured, perhaps he was dying, just as... She dared not think of it.

He put a hand to his forehead. 'Don't fuss, girl. Just tell Tubb to come up.'

'Tubb's not here,' she said, adding anxiously, 'I'm sure I should get a doctor.'

'I don't—want—a doctor,' he said slowly, as though to a child. 'All I need is a hot bath and a large whisky.'

He started to get up but she pushed him back. 'You stay here while I run a bath for you.' She decided to take charge.

He didn't argue and she went to the bathroom and filled the bath three-quarters full with steaming water. She switched on the electric towel-rail, fetched a warm dressing-gown from the wardrobe in Saul's room and hung it on the bathroom door. Then she returned to her own room.

He hadn't moved. 'All ready,' she said, trying to sound impersonal, like an efficient nurse. 'Come along.'

He waved her away irritably, but when he swayed on his feet and she put an arm round him and led him to the bathroom he gave in without argument.

Here he slumped on to the cork-covered stool. Nicola peeled off his wet coat and, after some difficulty, managed to get off his soaking shoes and socks.

'Can you manage the rest yourself?' she said brightly. 'I'll help if you like; I'm not shy.'

'I'll manage,' he said between gritted teeth and she knew how he hated feeling helpless.

She hurried down to the living-room and poured out a large measure of whisky. For a moment she hesitated outside the bathroom door and then went in without knocking. Saul was stretched out full-length under the steaming water. He rolled over hastily, frowning up at her. 'I didn't invite you to come in,' he said.

She smiled, humouring him. 'So you didn't. I brought you this.'

She held out the glass and a brown arm emerged from under the water and grasped it, muttering something that might have been thanks.

'There's a hot meal ready,' she said. 'Would you like to go straight to bed and I'll bring you a tray up?'

He took a gulp of whisky and actually grinned feebly at her. 'I'll come down,' he said. 'Now go away; you make me nervous.'

The sound of energetic splashing reached her as she went downstairs, carrying the pile of wet clothes. That was a good sign; it meant that Saul couldn't be seriously hurt.

In the kitchen she made a neat pile of the clothes and put them in a corner of the room for Tubb to cope with. She checked on the casserole in the oven. It smelled delicious. She loaded up a trolley and wheeled it to the living-room, where she set the table. Rain was still beating heavily against the window but the room looked cosy, with the parchment-shaded table lamp shining on polished silver and glittering crystal wine glasses, arranged on a white damask cloth. There were crusty rolls—probably baked by Tubb this morning—and a jug of cream, awaiting the arrival of the strawberries still in the fridge. She looked through the bottles of wine in the drinks cupboard and selected one that she thought might go with the chicken casserole, but Saul could approve that later. She put a couple of small logs on the fire and smiled as she saw that Bo'sun was curled up on the sofa, fast asleep.

She heard Saul speaking on the phone in his bedroom and a few minutes later he came downstairs. He was wearing the dressing-gown over a pair of grey trousers.

Nicola smiled at him encouragingly. 'You're looking much better. Are you ready for some food? Tubb left a chicken casserole in the oven.'

He sat down at the table, eyeing it appreciatively. 'Five-star service—*very* nice indeed! That's what I need now,' he said. 'Food—and some sparkling conversation.'

Nicola made an effort to reply lightly. 'I can promise the former,' she said over her shoulder as she went into the kitchen.

She put the dish on the table and held out the bottle of wine. 'Will that do?'

'Saint Estèphe, good choice,' he said, reading the label. 'And just the right temperature. Paul has trained you well.' He slanted her a teasing glance.

She ignored that and began to serve the casserole, while he filled their glasses. 'Now,' she said, 'won't you tell me what happened, please?'

He was economical with words. He'd just turned into the lane, in a torrent of rain, he failed to notice that a large tree was down across the road, probably struck by lightning. He had swerved, skidded, and ended up with the car lying on its side in the ditch, which was fast filling up with rain.

'I won't go into detail,' he went on, 'but, briefly, the door was jammed and it took me about half an hour to get out, and when I finally managed it I fell slap into the ditch—which explains my filthy condition when I burst in upon you.'

Nicola knew enough about Saul to guess that a gush of soft sympathy wouldn't be well-received. 'That was bad luck,' she said. 'It was a nasty storm.' Remembering it, she gave an involuntary shiver.

He met her eyes across the table. 'You're upset by storms? Was that why you were packing when I came in?'

She floundered. 'Well—yes—no—I mean yes to the first question, no to the second.'

'Then why?' he said softly. 'Tell me.'

Now was the time to bring out all the grievances she'd been rehearsing. She shrugged. 'It doesn't matter now.'

'I'd like to know,' he insisted.

'Yes, I dare say you would,' she retorted. 'And there are a great many things I'd like to know—but you won't tell me.'

'Fair enough,' he said, holding up his glass. 'Let's drink to the moment when all shall be revealed. When there are no more secrets between the two of us.'

Nicola sipped her wine. The two of us! Her eyes met his across the table—met and held. His mouth was tilted into an odd, whimsical smile, a smile that she had never seen before. He looked so fabulously attractive, she thought, and she couldn't suppress a small jolt of excitement. The lamplight threw shadows from his cheekbones down the hollows in his lean cheeks and the brilliant eyes, half closed, were like dark lakes. Stop it, she told herself crossly. You're not going to fall under his spell again. She said casually, 'It's a good thing Ros wasn't in the car with you.'

The dark brows lifted. 'Ros? Why should she be with me in the car?'

Nicola crumbled a roll. 'She came round here looking for you this morning. And then Eleanor told me she'd gone to London to meet you.'

'Well, I'm afraid she wasted her time. I haven't been at the office. I've been at The Wharf most of the day.'

The Wharf was a large building on the south side of the river, used by Jarrett's for storage of shipments of wine. Nicola had been there once with Paul and recalled the chill of the cellars with their close-packed racks of bottles, and the stuffy little office on the top floor where Terry Gurney, the store manager, dealt with the paperwork and customs requirements.

'Yes,' Saul was going on, 'I had a lot of things to discuss with Terry. There are——' He broke off, frowning. His mind was on his business worries.

But Nicola's mind was on what he had said about Ros—or rather what he hadn't said. He hadn't seemed at all put out that he had missed her.

'But don't let's talk about business just now,' he said. 'I've had my fill of business just lately. I was up half the night working—and all today. I want to enjoy this most delectable meal. Tubb's casseroles are quite something.'

Nicola agreed warmly. All at once she found she was enjoying her food. So he hadn't spent the night with Ros. Was it possible that she'd been wrong all along, and that Ros herself had been wrong too?

'Now tell me,' Saul said as strawberries and cream replaced the casserole, 'what you've been doing with yourself all day—before the storm struck, that is. I hope you've been missing me.' His dark eyes danced mischievously.

'Oh, I've been much too busy to miss you. Tubb looked after me beautifully. I sat out on the veranda and read for a while and Bo'sun kept me company. Then I went for a lovely walk in the lane. Then Tubb gave me a splendid lunch, and then Eleanor looked in to see me. Oh, by the way, she came to say that she's having a drinks party tomorrow evening and she wants us both to go. The idea is, I believe, to present me to the neighbours. She seemed specially thrilled to have induced Sir Victor Wells, the local celebrity, to come along.' Saul had grimaced at the idea of a party, but he brightened up at the mention of Sir Victor.

'Oh, good, there'll be someone intelligent to talk to. He's a great chap, our Sir Victor, and a superb conductor. Have you heard of him?'

They talked music happily over the strawberries and cream and then Nicola stood up. 'I'll go and make coffee,' she said, starting to push back the sofa to where it had formerly stood.

Saul put a hand on hers. 'Let's leave it where it is. The room looks so cosy, with the rain shut out and the fire burning cheerfully. The perfect end to the day for the overworked businessman.' He pulled the low table up beside the sofa and sat down, stretching out his long legs with a contented sigh.

In the kitchen Nicola stood watching the coffee percolate and her spirits bubbled up in unison with the dark liquid in the flask. She was beginning to believe that perhaps Saul wasn't in love with Ros and that his mysterious need of a fiancée wasn't a deep-laid plot to lure Ros back to him.

From the living-room came the sound of music. She recognised a Spanish piece—she couldn't remember the name. She gazed down at the ring on her engagement finger, the stones glittering in the brilliant light from the overhead fitting. It was still only a fake, she reminded herself.

She carried the tray in and set it on the low table beside the sofa. 'I remembered I had a disc of *Nights in the Gardens of Spain* by de Falla, with Sir Victor conducting,' Saul told her.

'Lovely,' Nicola said automatically. She noticed that he had switched off the table lamp and now there was only firelight in the room. Soft light and sweet music, she thought uneasily and began to stack up the dishes on the dinner-table.

'Leave that, Tubb will clear them,' Saul told her imperiously. He reached out and caught hold of the skirt of her dress. 'Come and sit down and be restful.' He moved until he could grab her arm, and pulled her down on to the sofa beside him. His hand remained, resting round her shoulders. She felt suddenly shy, but she didn't move away. He said, 'That was a beastly storm. Were you very frightened?'

She laughed unsteadily. 'Terrified! I shook like a jelly all the time. I was expecting a thunderbolt to come down the chimney at any moment. Bo'sun was terrified too,' she added, reaching out to stroke Bo'sun's head as he lay fast asleep at the other end of the sofa.

Saul drew her closer and rested his cheek against her hair. 'I wish I'd been here,' he said softly.

Nicola tried to keep the atmosphere light. 'You couldn't be here as you were sitting in a ditch,' she reminded him.

'Too true! And when I managed to extricate myself all I could do was to burst in on you looking like something washed up by the tide and then bawl you out when you tried to help me. I'm sorry.'

'Oh, that didn't matter, so long as you weren't badly hurt. I didn't mean to fuss, but I'm—I'm inclined to over-react about road accidents—and that was the first thing that came into my mind when I saw you. I thought you might be dying.'

She stared into the fire and her eyes blurred. 'I lost both my parents in a car crash when I was a baby, you see. Did Gran tell you?' She added in a forlorn little voice, 'I don't remember them at all.' She pulled a handkerchief from her cardigan pocket and blew her nose. 'Sorry,' she gulped.

Saul put a hand under her chin and turned her face towards him, gently brushing away two large tears that had settled on her cheeks. 'Dear little Nikki,' he said huskily. 'I like you very much.'

She knew he was going to kiss her and she knew that she wanted him to. It had been such a ghastly day; she felt as if she'd been carrying a huge weight around with her. But now it had gone and she was floating free as air. It was heaven to be here, with Saul's arm around her. She closed her eyes as his mouth came down on hers.

His lips were warm as they moved on her mouth and smelled of wine and strawberries. It was a playful kiss. He kissed her eyes, one at a time, then his lips buried themselves in the hollow of her neck. She felt languid and slightly intoxicated. Lifting a hand to his shoulder, she found that his dressing-gown had fallen open and her fingers encountered the smooth, moist skin of his neck and the tangle of hair that ran down his chest. She felt him shudder and his other arm went round her and held her hard against him. His kiss became more urgent, his tongue moving along the line of her lips. When it thrust into her mouth she felt as if she was going to faint. As the tension built up between them she clung to him, giving him back kiss for kiss, her fingers digging into the thick hair at the back of his neck.

'Darling Nikki,' he muttered close to her ear, 'couldn't we both drown our sorrows together? It's a fiancé's privilege, you know.'

It was as if he'd thrown a bucket of cold water over her. 'No,' she cried, pushing at his chest. 'No.'

'Why not?' he pleaded.

'I'm not your fiancée, that's why.'

His grip slackened and she edged quickly away from him along the sofa and hit up against Bo'sun's sleeping body. Rudely awakened, he let out an affronted yelp and jumped down on to the hearthrug, where he sat looking dazed, licking one paw as if he'd been mortally wounded. The absurd little incident made Nicola want to burst into wild laughter. She slipped down beside Bo'sun and petted him apologetically.

Saul hadn't moved and when Nicola glanced up at him she couldn't see his expression in the flickering light of the fire. Neither of them spoke. Only the soft Spanish music sounded in the room, for what seemed an interminable time.

Finally, with a muttered exclamation, Saul stood up and switched off the hi-fi. The silence in the room was complete. He poured out some coffee and banged the cup down in disgust. 'It's cold,' he said.

Nicola scrambled to her feet. 'I'll make some more,' she said, picking up the tray.

He grabbed her wrist and forced the tray down again on the table. 'Leave it,' he said curtly. 'Now you'd better go to bed.'

She straightened up. 'Don't you dare treat me like a child,' she said. By now she was seething with anger.

'If you behave like a child then what do you expect?' His voice was icy. 'If you treated Paul the way you've just treated me I'm not surprised he ditched you.'

This was too much. 'May I remind you...' Nicola tried to sound dignified but her voice was shaking '...that it was you who set up the great seduction scene?' She waved a hand vaguely to the fire, the sofa, the hi-fi, the lamp switched off. 'And if it went wrong you've only got yourself to blame. I'm going to bed now, and I'm leaving in the morning, as I told you earlier. Nothing that has happened this evening has made me change my mind.'

She turned to stalk out of the room but Saul was after her in a flash. He caught her by the shoulders and twirled her round. 'No girl speaks to me like that,' he snarled.

'Oh, yes, they do,' she flashed back. 'I just have.' They were both blazingly angry by now.

'Not without paying for it.' He pulled her roughly against him, so tightly that she couldn't breathe, and his mouth came down on hers in a hard kiss that went on and on.

When he finally released her she took a step back and slapped him across the cheek as hard as she could.

Then she ran out of the room and upstairs, locking her bedroom door behind her.

CHAPTER EIGHT

THAT night Nicola lay awake for hour after hour. She tossed and turned, thumped her pillow, wept a good deal and got colder and colder until at last she got up to search for an extra blanket. Fortunately she found one in the bottom drawer of the dressing-chest. If she hadn't she doubted if she would have had any sleep at all. She had had a night like this when Keith had finally left her. The circumstances were quite different but the lump of heavy misery in her chest was just the same.

She was in love with Saul Jarrett and she had to face the fact that she had allowed herself to hope that he was beginning to care for her. Tonight he'd shown her, in two short sentences, exactly what he thought of her. However much he had pretended in these last few days to like and even admire her, what he had said had proved that he was merely using her as a diversion in this game he was playing. And, worse, that he was still suspicious of her motives. Her cheeks burned as she remembered his words to Paul at that fatal meeting in the study where it all began. He'd said that he didn't have to dangle a wedding-ring as bait to get a girl into his bed. Yes, that was what he'd said. She was filled with helpless anger at the injustice of it and the impossibility of trying to explain to him, without giving herself and her feelings away.

No, she had to get away; she would become a gibbering wreck if she stayed here any longer. She assured herself that she would get over Saul in time, just as she'd got over Keith.

She got up and washed her face, wrapped herself in the blanket, pulled the duvet up to her chin, and gave herself a sensible talking-to. By the time she finally fell asleep she had made her plans for the next morning.

The plans went wrong from the start. She had set her little travelling alarm clock for six o'clock but when she finally awoke the sun was streaming in round the curtains and it was nearly ten. She must have slept right through the alarm for the first time in her life. Oh, well, perhaps there was no harm done, she thought. Her plan would just be put forward an hour or two.

Holding tightly to her resolution, she got up and dressed, packed everything in her bag and carried it down to the hall—quite openly, not creeping round corners trying to evade Saul. She hoped she wouldn't meet him, but if she did she had her words all ready and whatever he said there was no way he could stop her leaving unless he locked her up, and that wouldn't suit his purpose. Apparently he had to have a fiancée on show.

There was a clattering of dishes from the kitchen and Nicola decided to enlist Tubb's help to order a taxi. She pushed open the kitchen door—and stopped dead.

Saul, with a tea-towel tucked into his trousers, was piling their dinner plates into the dishwasher. He looked round when he heard her and smiled. 'Good morning, Nikki. Had a good sleep? Never mind—it's Sunday. And a lovely morning after the storm.'

Just as if nothing had happened! It was unbelievable. She stood frozen.

'I've kept some coffee hot for you,' he went on cheerfully, 'and there's rolls and butter and marmalade on the table over there. I usually have breakfast here on Sunday. Tubb stays overnight with his sister on Saturdays. He'll be in around midday.'

Nicola felt paralysed. She licked her dry lips and said stupidly, 'But you told me last night that Tubb would clear away the dishes.'

'Did I?' said Saul, going to the Aga, where the coffee-flask was standing on the warming plate. He grinned. 'Well, he couldn't, could he, because he wasn't here.' He poured coffee into a mug and carried it across the room to her. 'Come and sit down and have something to eat and I'll tell you my plans for the day.'

She still didn't move but she couldn't resist taking a gulp of the coffee, which was too hot and burnt her mouth. Oh, no, she wasn't going to let him get away with this. She said stiffly, 'I happen to have plans of my own.'

He finished rinsing the sink and came towards her, drying his hands and throwing the tea-towel aside. 'Oh, yes?' he enquired suavely.

'Yes,' she repeated, gathering strength. 'I told you I intended to leave this morning, and I am. I thought Tubb was here and I came in to ask him to tell me where to ring for a taxi to take me to the station.'

He burst out laughing. 'Still wanting to be taken to the station! I thought you would have recovered from that minor neurosis by now.'

She held her ground sturdily. 'I'm serious, Saul. I've made up my mind.'

He stood in silence, studying her face and she met his eyes without flinching. She said, 'I'm sorry I can't help you with your scheme—whatever it is—but the situation here has become intolerable and I'm not going to stay any longer.'

His face had changed. His mouth became a hard line and she could see a glint of anger in his dark eyes. She felt fear curling in her stomach but she stood her ground. 'Perhaps you would ring for a taxi for me.'

'You certainly won't get a taxi in these parts on a Sunday morning,' Saul said, so definitely that she had to believe him. 'I'm afraid you'll have to trust me to drive you to the station.'

She eyed him suspiciously. 'I thought your car was in a ditch. Are you planning to drive the Rolls?'

'No, I'm not,' Saul said shortly. 'I have a hired car at my disposal. It was delivered earlier.'

'Then if there's no taxi I think I'll walk,' Nicola said.

Saul stuck his hands in his pockets and surveyed her thoughtfully. She recognised that look—he was plotting something. 'The station's over four miles away,' he said smoothly. 'I hope your bag isn't too heavy.'

Nicola's heart sank. Her bag was extremely heavy and she hadn't forgotten the walk she'd had yesterday morning. She said, 'Will you give me your word to take me to the station?'

Having won his point, Saul relaxed and placed one hand on his chest. 'Cross my heart,' he said. 'Are you ready to leave now?'

He didn't argue or question her. Probably he'd decided that his mysterious scheme wasn't worth the trouble of putting up with a naïve young girl whom he'd had to go to the trouble of charming in order to get his own way. Or perhaps he'd got what he wanted. Perhaps it had been Ros all the time.

'Let's go, then,' he said, taking a light jacket from the back of a chair and slinging it over his shoulder. He picked up her bag and stowed it in the boot of an open two-seater white sports car which stood in the drive. 'OK? You haven't left anything behind?' he said, opening the door for her.

Only my heart, she thought.

'No, nothing,' she said tightly as he got in beside her.

Saul started the engine and the sports car zoomed down the drive at a tremendous speed. 'I'll have to go the long way round to the station,' Saul said, raising his voice, 'in case they haven't lifted the tree yet.' After that he didn't speak another word.

There was very little traffic on the main road, where yesterday the rush of cars had been continuous. It seemed to Nicola that they reached the British Rail sign to the station approach road almost before they started.

The car pulled up outside the entrance. The doors were all shut and there was nobody about. 'You're out of luck, my girl,' Saul said, hardly bothering to hide his satisfaction.

Nicola reached out to open the door. It was locked. 'I'm quite prepared to wait,' she said. 'Will you please unlock the door?'

He hadn't switched off the engine. 'I think yours is a rotten plan,' he said. 'So we'll try my plan instead.' He let in the clutch, stepped on the accelerator and the powerful car leapt forward across the station yard and out into the main road.

'Stop,' Nicola screeched. 'Let me get out.'

He didn't appear to hear. Her eyes went to the speed-ometer. Fifty—sixty—seventy. Nicola gave up her first thought of jumping out over the side of the open car and looked about her for possible ways of escape. Cows on the road, or sheep, would force Saul to stop. But no farm animals appeared. She gave up any hope of escape for the moment. Saul hadn't driven through the village and they appeared to be travelling in open country. Signposts flashed past too quickly for her to decipher them. She held on to the edge of her seat, praying that Saul would slow down.

After another five or six miles had whizzed past the road became twisty, and Saul drew into a lay-by and switched off the engine. He gave the wheel a loving pat. 'I admit she's a little noisy,' he said. 'But, my God, what speed! What acceleration!'

Nicola drew a long, exasperated breath but before she could explode into fury Saul touched her hand and she was reduced to silence by a sudden tightening of her throat. 'Don't say it, Nikki. I couldn't just let you walk out on me like that and you didn't seem open to reason while we were in the house.'

'You knew,' she accused him hotly. 'You tricked me. You knew the station would be closed on Sunday morning.'

'That's not quite true. I *hoped* it would be.'

'Oh,' she sneered, 'and what would you have done if it had been open and I'd just walked away into the train?'

'I'd have bought a ticket and come with you. I'd have come with you anywhere you went. You don't think I'd have broken my promise to Gran, do you?'

He would have done too, she admitted to herself. All her careful planning was a waste of time. This man would get the better of her whatever she did. She turned her back on him and looked out over the fields, green and sparkling after the rain last night.

Saul said quietly, 'Don't you think you'd better tell me what all this is about? I seem to remember that you'd made up your mind to leave before I got in last night, so I can't believe it's all because of my suggestion that you should—er—share my bed. Anyway, you wanted it as much as I did, didn't you, Nikki? Didn't you?' he repeated fiercely when she didn't reply.

'No, I didn't. I . . .' She bit her lip. How could she possibly explain to him that it was because she was in love with him and he wasn't in love with her, that was why?

'Oh, never mind, let it go,' he said impatiently. 'But I want an explanation of why you intended to break your promise. I'm sorry if you've been bored because I haven't been here to entertain you. My business——'

'Oh, don't be idiotic, Saul,' she broke in. 'Don't you know me better than that?'

He smiled faintly. 'I thought I did. I took you for rather a self-sufficient young lady. Well, then, tell me why.'

She was on safer ground now. 'Because I had an absolutely horrible day. First of all I was attacked by your cousin Ros, who was insulting——'

'Ros?' Saul broke in. 'What was she complaining about?'

Nicola thought quickly. 'She doesn't like me and she wanted to get rid of me. She made me really angry so I went out to walk it off and I had a long trek in the boiling sun, all among the traffic.'

'You told me you'd had a lovely walk,' Saul put in.

'Well, it wasn't,' she snapped.

'Go on,' he said quietly.

He really was giving her his full attention now. 'Soon after I got back Eleanor carried on with the attack. She wants to get rid of me too, only she's not so straightforward as Ros. She's disgustingly patronising and she works in an underhand way, with hints and smiles...'

'Yes, I know,' Saul said feelingly.

'Then there was the storm and I was all alone and— and——' her voice faltered but she pulled herself together again '—and I was as much in the dark as ever about what I was supposed to be doing. And I just felt I couldn't take any more of it.' Miserably aware that she sounded like a spoilt child, in this recital of her grievances, she added forcibly, 'And I didn't see why I should.'

She turned her head again and looked towards the fields. There was a long silence. Three cars passed by. A black and white cow ambled up and surveyed them with interest over the hedge, munching contentedly.

At last Saul said slowly, 'Yes—I see. I've been thoughtless. Look, Nikki, I'll make a bargain with you. Give me until the end of the week—next Saturday—and then, come what may, we'll cancel our—er—arrangement. I'll fix up for you to stay somewhere away from the Manor so that you won't need to go back to Watford until I'm quite sure that it's safe to do so. In any case, I don't approve of your being there alone.'

Approve! Nicola fumed inwardly. She didn't care whether he approved or not; she would please herself.

'I could take you up to stay at my country club for a week or two,' Saul went on thoughtfully. 'It's in Warwickshire. I think you'd like it.' He paused for a moment and then went on in a voice which touched her because of its deep seriousness, 'This is very important to me, Nikki, more important, even, than it was at first.'

She swallowed. 'All right then. Until the end of the week—that's a promise?'

'A promise,' he said gravely. He held out his hand. 'Friends?'

'Friends,' she echoed. She had to put her hand into his and its firm pressure awakened all the magic more potently than ever.

He kept her hand in his, smiling into her eyes. 'Thank you, Nikki,' he said in the deep voice that sent shivers up and down her spine. Then he released her hand abruptly and switched on the car ignition.

As the car joined the road again Saul said, 'We're having lunch with some friends of mine who have a cottage in Sussex, about fifteen miles or so from here. Lucy and Tom Felton are quite delightful. I think you'll find them a decided improvement on the company at Pemberton Manor,' he added drily. 'Tom is an electronics wizard and he's recently landed a top job in the US. They're moving soon; I'll miss them.'

'Will they expect us to be engaged?' Nicola enquired.

'Oh, yes, indeed. They're delighted,' he said. Keeping his eyes on the road, he groped for her left hand. 'You're not wearing your ring.' His voice sharpened. 'What have you done with it?'

She pulled her hand away quickly. He probably thought she'd hurled it into the bushes in a fit of pique. 'Don't worry,' she said, 'I've got it here.' She opened her handbag and felt for the little ring-box. 'I intended to hand it back to you before I left but I suppose I'll have to wear it for a few days more.' She took the ring out of its box and slipped it on to her finger. It felt oddly at home there now; in fact her finger had felt quite bare without it.

Saul gave a grunt of approval. As the car gained speed again Nicola glanced up at him. His dark hair was ruffled in the breeze. His eyes were narrowed on the road ahead and a faint smile played round his lips. He looked— smug, she thought crossly. He'd got his own way and won her over and now he could forget all about her and enjoy his love-affair with a motor car. How like a man, she thought with new-found cynicism.

Nicola had never driven in a car like this before. She guessed that, with all the power that was stowed away under the bonnet, it would be tricky to handle. However, after those first hair-raising miles, when she'd gripped the edge of her seat in terror, Saul now seemed content to keep within reasonable limits. So she sat back, enjoyed the feeling of the cool air on her hot cheeks and watched the countryside, with its neat fields and great trees and tiny villages. She'd never been in Sussex before and it appealed to her now as being typically English.

Presently she saw the shape of hills in the distance, hazy in the sunshine. 'Ah!' she cried. 'Those must be the South Downs.'

'They certainly are,' Saul agreed. 'You know this part of the world?'

'Not at all, but it's very attractive.'

'I love it,' he said with emphasis and it was the first time she had heard real enthusiasm in his voice.

He slowed the car down so that she could hear him above the noise of the engine. 'My grandmother lived in these parts,' he said. 'I used to visit her quite often when I was at school. It was such a relief to get away from the Manor. I used to walk miles upon the Downs. You feel as if you're on top of the world.'

Soon he turned the car off the road and drove slowly along a maze of narrow lanes, eventually stopping before a long, low cottage built of brick and half timbered. It had the appearance of nestling in a glade, with massive trees to right and left and in front a garden rioting with delphiniums and poppies and all kinds of summer flowers.

Saul didn't turn into the short drive. Instead he drew the car on to a grassy patch. 'Hill Cottage,' he said, with a kind of satisfaction, as if he were showing off some rare treasure.

'What a lovely home,' Nicola said. 'I don't know how your friends can bear to leave it.'

'Neither do I,' he admitted. And then spoilt it by adding with a shrug, 'You have to go where the money is.'

A young woman in a green gingham dress came running out of the cottage, dark curls flying round rosy cheeks. 'Saul—why are you sitting there? Why don't you

come in? And what showy monster is this?' She placed
a finger on the white bonnet of the sports car.

'Nice little job, isn't she?' Saul vaulted over the side
of the car. 'Hello, Lucy, dear,' he said and kissed her.

He came round and opened the passenger door for
Nicola. Lucy didn't wait to be introduced. She took both
Nicola's hands and kissed her, then stood back sur-
veying her. 'So,' she said, brown eyes dancing, 'you're
the girl this choosy old individual has managed to
capture.' She pulled a face at Saul. 'Oh, yes, Saul, you
know you are.'

Before he could reply to this taunt a tall, thin man
with fair hair and a long, clever face came towards them
and this time Nicola was properly introduced to Tom
Felton, who shook hands with them both heartily.

'Come along in,' Lucy bubbled. 'I've set lunch in the
garden as it's such a lovely day. And don't we deserve
it after last night? What a storm! Did you have it in your
part of the world? I thought the thatch was going to
catch fire.'

Chatting away, she led them through the cottage and
into the garden, where a table was set for lunch in the
shade of a silver-birch tree.

Nicola stood still, exclaiming with delight at the view
in front of her. The lawn sloped down gently into an
unseen valley, beyond which the land rose with dramatic
steepness, up and up into a vivid blue sky. The tiny shape
of a horse looked like a child's toy, as did the sheep that
were dotted about in twos and threes, pale against the
green of the hillside.

Beside Nicola, Lucy waved a proprietorial hand. 'Our
view,' she announced proudly.

Nicola drew in a breath. 'It's stunning. Like the
backdrop of some gigantic stage-set.'

'That's what I always think,' Lucy agreed. 'Now come and sit down and I'll bring lunch out.'

As lunch went on Nicola found she was enjoying herself. It was pleasant to eat delicious food, with home-grown salad and fruit, and she liked her hosts immediately—Lucy so charming and vivacious, Tom, quiet and wryly humorous. But what added most to her enjoyment was the difference in Saul. Here, with his friends, he was another man altogether from the one she thought she knew. He was easy, relaxed. The creases had gone from his forehead, he laughed at Lucy's teasing and listened with obvious enthusiasm as Tom expounded the latest electronic marvels he was working on. Gone was the sardonic expression he usually wore when he was at Pemberley Manor.

Lunch was a leisurely affair, and afterwards they lingered, talking lazily, enjoying the pleasure of having eaten well, in congenial company. Before it was time to leave, Lucy showed Nicola over the cottage. 'It's what the agents call "deceptively spacious",' she said with her little chuckle. 'Actually it was originally three farm workers' cottages but it was completely revamped by the people who lived here before us. They did it rather well, I've always thought. I like the little passages and the window-seats, and the views they managed to arrange from all the windows.' She sighed rather wistfully. 'I'll hate leaving it to someone else. But we've been here nearly ten years and time moves on. America will be great fun, I'm sure.' She cheered up at the thought.

The visit ended all too soon for Nicola, especially as Saul reminded her of Eleanor's party, which she wasn't looking forward to at all. But presently they were back on the road, Saul having promised faithfully to bring Nicola to see them again before they left for America. A chill struck her as she realised that it was a promise he had no intention of keeping. At the end of the week their 'engagement' would be over.

His voice broke in on her thoughts. 'Well, what did you think of Hill Cottage?'

'It's heaven,' Nicola said simply and he seemed pleased when she added that she'd liked his friends and thanked him for taking her. 'Although I felt rather a fraud for deceiving them,' she added. 'They seem such sincere, straightforward people.'

'Implying that I'm not?' The mockery was back in his voice; Saul was himself again and all her pleasure in the lovely afternoon had gone. She made no reply and after that they didn't exchange another word until they arrived back at the Manor. Here he deposited her at the front door, saying that he would see her later, he was going to find out if the garage man had got his car out of the ditch yet.

Left alone, facing the massive, tightly closed door, Nicola reflected disgustedly that the afternoon had not improved his manners, and made her way round the side of the house to enter by way of the veranda. She felt as if she was entering by the servants' entrance. That, she thought, with a twisted smile, was entirely appropriate.

Nicola usually enjoyed dressing for a party but as she dried her hair after a refreshing shower she knew that this evening was an exception. Even the prospect of meeting Sir Victor Wells, the conductor, whose work she so much admired, didn't cheer her up. She had a dark suspicion that the party had been arranged solely for the purpose of making her feel out of place and inadequate among Eleanor's up-market friends. It was, in a way, amusing to reflect that all Eleanor's poison darts, intended to cause a rift between Nicola and Saul, had been futile. The rift had been there at the beginning and would remain to the end. She'd seen a genuinely warmer and more pleasant side to him when he was with his friends this afternoon, but it hadn't changed her belief that he saw her with the same cynicism with which he seemed to view most of the world. He would certainly misinterpret any effort on her part to dress up to please him.

With all this in mind she chose a simple linen dress of a clear pale blue, a shade lighter than her eyes, and her only ornament was a blue enamel pendant on a slim silver chain, which had been Gran's twenty-first birthday present to her.

When she was ready she stood before the long mirror and was pleased with the result. Her skin was fresh and clear and a careful application of shadow and mascara added depth to the blue of her eyes. She brushed her hair until it fell with a glossy sheen nearly to her shoulders, where it curved outwards. Yes, she looked exactly the way she was—an ordinary, reasonably pretty girl with no nonsense about her. A serious girl, was what Saul had called her and she supposed she was, at least about the important things. And yet there was a glint of mischief that looked back at her as she thought suddenly that, in an odd way, she was in fact almost looking forward to this party. Perhaps that was because she had nothing to lose from Eleanor's plotting. She was still wearing Saul's ring but she wasn't going to put on an act any longer. She would just be herself from now on.

She heard Saul's step on the stairs and the slam of his bedroom door behind him, followed by sundry thumps and bangs, indicative of a man dressing for a party in a hurry. Nicola smiled to herself and sat down to wait.

He was very quick. Not more than ten minutes later he knocked at her door. 'Are you there, Nikki—are you ready?'

She opened the door to him. 'Quite ready.'

She looked him up and down coolly. One of his shirt buttons was unfastened and there was a small gash on his chin.

'You've cut yourself,' she said. 'You're going to bleed on to your collar if you're not careful.'

He swore comprehensively and dived back into his bedroom, to emerge with a small circular plaster on his chin.

'That's better,' Nicola said. Then she gave herself the dangerous pleasure of leaning nearer to fasten the button.

'Be careful, Nikki,' he said, sniffing at the perfume of her newly washed hair, 'or we shan't be going to that party at all.'

She stepped back quickly. 'I thought you want to advertise to the neighbourhood that you've got a fiancée,' she said. 'Isn't that what I'm supposed to be for?'

He followed her down the stairs. 'Don't needle me, Nikki,' he growled. 'I've had a hell of a time helping my friend from the garage to hoist my car out of the ditch. And now I need a whisky before we go in...'

He went into the living-room and emerged with a glass in one hand and an enormous box of chocolates in the other. He held it out to her. 'This is for you,' he said. 'It's been sitting in the car all night. I couldn't get it out. It doesn't look any the worse for it.'

He tossed down the whisky while Nicola stammered her thanks. The gesture had taken her by surprise. She'd been nursing all sorts of grudges against him yesterday and yet he'd found time to buy her a present.

He put down his glass and took her arm. 'Come along; we'd better go and join the fray.'

Nicola left her box of chocolates on the hall table and walked with him into the main house and across the hall to the drawing-room, where she saw at once that her guess had been right. The guests had been specially picked, she was sure, to demonstrate to Saul how out of place she was among people of his own social standing.

Certainly, it was like no party Nicola had ever been to. You wouldn't need to shriek to make yourself heard above the din. There was no din, only a muted flow of conversation, punctuated occasionally by a well-modulated laugh or a deep bass guffaw. You wouldn't have to squeeze your elbows into your sides so that you could convey a glass to your mouth without danger. There was plenty of space to move around.

The women were sleek and sophisticated and expensively dressed in understated couturier styles. The men, mostly gathered round a groaning buffet table at the end of the room, fairly oozed with *bonhomie* and fat bank balances.

No doubt about it, Eleanor had chosen her guests with care and she was moving among them, regal in her black velvet and pearls, with a self-satisfied air of belonging intimately to this top stratum of society.

She saw Nicola and Saul standing in the doorway and glided up to them. 'Come along, children. Saul, dear, go and find Nicola a drink while I introduce her to people.'

'Introduce', Nicola felt, wasn't the right word. 'Exhibited' would have been a better one. Eleanor's formula didn't vary. 'I'd like you to meet Saul's new fiancée, such a sweet girl.' Nicola promptly forgot their names. They smiled at her graciously and wished her happiness and eyed her up and down in her simple linen dress, clearly wondering where Saul Jarrett had picked her up and how such a pathetic nonentity had managed to capture the most eligible bachelor in the neighbourhood. She began to feel that a false smile was being glued on her mouth and she looked round for Saul, who had been buttonholed by Toby at the buffet table, and was engaged in conversation. But eventually he appeared at her side with a glass of champagne and she sipped it slowly, taking care not to get the bubbles up her nose and disgrace herself.

'Keep it up,' Saul murmured in her ear. 'You've got the men frothing at the mouth.'

She pulled a face at him. 'How unutterably vulgah,' she giggled, and saw Saul's understanding grin. It was refreshing to share a joke with him and he seemed to see the funny side of this party.

Nicola saw Tubb standing in the doorway, making signals, and put a hand on Saul's arm. 'I think Tubb's trying to attract your attention,' she said.

He let out a small, explosive curse. 'I've been half expecting a phone call. I'll have to desert you for the moment, Nikki. I'll be back as soon as I can.'

She watched him stride away through the throng and wondered if she could decently go after him. She looked round for Eleanor and saw her talking to a tall, thin man, who had evidently just arrived. Sir Victor Wells, undoubtedly. Although Nicola only knew him at a distance and mostly from the back as he conducted the orchestra, she couldn't mistake that distinguished figure with the slightly waving grey hair and neatly trimmed beard. As he turned she had a full view of his face and saw the wide forehead and shrewd, kind eyes, and thought what a wonderful man he must be to have all that superb musical knowledge and sensitivity.

He seemed to know most of the guests and he went round, shaking hands and exchanging a word here and there. Nicola put aside the temptation to follow Saul. She'd been a fan of Sir Victor's for ages and she couldn't forgo the pleasure of actually meeting him.

So she stayed where she was until Eleanor came to her side. 'Where's Saul got to?' she enquired. She was obviously annoyed.

'He had to go off and take a phone call,' Nicola said.

'Oh, well——' Eleanor shrugged. 'You'd better come and meet Sir Victor. Do your best,' she added patronisingly.

It was the same formula as usual, except that Eleanor managed to infuse an almost apologetic note into her voice. 'Sir Victor, may I introduce Nicola Oldfield, Saul's new fiancée?' She smiled up at him and said facetiously, 'Now is your chance to win one of the younger generation over to real music.' She gave her high, tinkling laugh, as if she realised, too late, what a silly joke that was.

Sir Victor was looking very strangely at Nicola, holding her hand in his. 'Nicola Oldfield? Are you by any wonderful chance related to Leon Oldfield, the violinist, who died so tragically many years ago?'

'He was my father,' Nicola said.

Sir Victor's face broke into a slow smile of incredulous pleasure. 'My dear, dear girl. This is a happy coincidence! I've often wondered about you.' He glanced at Eleanor. 'Nicola's father was one of my greatest friends. We were at the Royal College together and later played in the same orchestra. We were planning to start our own string quartet when he was killed in a car accident.' He bit his lip and shook his grey head. 'It was a great blow to me. He was a brilliant violinist—much better than I was.'

He turned back to Nicola. 'We must have a long talk, my dear.'

'Oh, yes, please,' Nicola said, quite stunned by this delightful surprise.

At that moment Saul returned and the two men shook hands while Sir Victor, obviously stirred by this unexpected meeting, began to tell Saul about it.

Nicola saw that Eleanor was furious that her cherished plan had misfired. Bright spots of colour had appeared on her cheekbones and her fingers were clenched tightly round the stem of the wine glass she held. She kept putting in little playful remarks which neither of the men was listening to. It was obvious that she intended to stay and find out if there was any hope of turning the situation to her advantage.

Sir Victor, his eyes twinkling with pleasure, clapped Saul on the back. 'This is a doubly happy occasion, my boy. I'm off to the Far East next week on a tour but when I return I must send you both tickets for a concert and we can have a proper celebration. That is, if Nicola can tolerate my kind of music,' he added with a sly glance in Eleanor's direction.

'Oh, indeed,' Nicola said. 'I haven't missed a single one of your London concerts in the last five years.'

They all laughed at that and Nicola could feel Eleanor's baffled anger taking firmer hold of her every moment.

'And when do you plan to get married?' Sir Victor enquired.

Saul's arm tightened round Nicola's shoulder as he replied, 'Oh, very soon. We're off to France tomorrow for a few days and as soon as we come back we plan to settle the day. Not more than a fortnight ahead, I believe, as soon as Nicola's grandmother gets back from a visit to Australia.'

With a sudden intake of breath, Eleanor started back, collided with a passing guest and lurched forward, emptying the entire contents of her glass of red wine over Nicola's dress.

In the moment of dismayed silence that followed Nicola saw Eleanor's face.

It had not been an accident. Staring down at the dark red stain spreading over the pale blue linen, she had a sick feeling that Eleanor would not have cared, at that moment, if it had been blood.

CHAPTER NINE

IGNORING cries of dismay and offers of help, Nicola fled. Out of the room, across the hall, and along the passage to Saul's front door, which was locked. She pressed the push button, praying that Tubb was in. He was and he didn't waste any words. Taking in the situation at a glance, he said practically, 'Just put your dress outside the bedroom door upstairs, miss. I'll see to it.'

Murmuring thanks, Nicola ran upstairs. By now the wine had soaked through to her skin and she felt cold and clammy. She stripped off all her clothes and rolled them into a bundle which she put outside the door. Then, with a sigh of thankfulness, she stepped under the shower.

When she was quite sure that her skin was free from every drop of wine, she lingered for a few minutes under the warm shower, relaxing, trying to put out of her mind the look on Eleanor's face.

Finally she dried, wrapped herself in a pink bath-towel and went into the bedroom to get a dressing-gown.

Saul was sitting in the cane bedroom chair, looking much too large for it. Nicola gave a little squeal and pulled the towel more closely round her. 'How dare you come into my room without knocking?' she demanded, edging towards the wardrobe.

She clutched the towel with one hand while she reached along the rail for her dressing-gown.

Saul stood up. 'I came to see if you were all right,' he said. 'I did knock but there was no answer so I came in to wait.'

'Well, I'm perfectly all right,' Nicola snapped, 'so you can go out again.' She had located the dressing-gown now and was struggling to get if off its hanger without releasing her hold on the towel.

He came up behind her. 'Let me help,' he said, taking the dressing-gown from her. 'You're getting in a terrible mess. Don't be silly, Nikki,' he remonstrated as she jumped away from him. 'I'm not going to leap on you.'

She turned her back and let the towel drop and then held her breath. But there was only a moment's hesitation before he was helping her arms into the sleeves of the gown.

She pulled it tightly round her. 'Now—out!' She glared up at him like a small avenging angel.

'You have a very beautiful back,' Saul said mildly.

'Out!' Nicola shouted.

'OK, OK.' He went towards the door. 'I'll wait downstairs while you find another dress to put on, then we'll go back to the party.'

'I am not,' Nicola said very distinctly, 'going back to the party.'

He raised dark eyebrows. 'Why not? Sir Victor is longing to talk to you.'

'And I'm longing to talk to him, but not now. Not here.'

'Oh, come on, Nikki.' He was beginning to sound irritated now. 'I'll buy you another dress. Don't make a big thing out of an accident.'

She looked steadily into his eyes. 'It wasn't an accident,' she said slowly and emphatically.

'But surely...' he began. 'Eleanor was full of apologies.'

'It wasn't an accident,' she repeated. She turned away, biting her lip, and added in a low voice, 'She hates me.

I—I know she's nothing to me and it shouldn't matter but—but somehow it does.'

There was a long silence. Then Saul came up behind her and put his arms round her, pulling her against him. 'I see,' he said slowly. 'I didn't understand. But it isn't you she hates, you know, it's me.'

He pressed his chin on top of her damp hair. 'I've been so damned busy and worried—I didn't realise what was going on here and I've let you bear the brunt of it. I'm sorry, Nikki; it's not been fair on you. I should never have started this thing, but at the time it seemed like a good idea. I'm sorry,' he said again.

His voice was so gentle and there was such genuine regret in it that Nicola felt the tears sting behind her eyes. She blinked them back, letting herself relish the bliss of feeling his arms around her, his breath warm on her cheek. For a long moment they stood motionless. Then he sighed and dropped his arms. 'I'll make your apologies to Sir Victor,' he said. 'I'll say you have a headache and tell him we'll be in touch when he comes back from his tour.'

Nicola thought bleakly that by then she and Saul would have said goodbye forever, but she let the remark pass.

'You make yourself comfortable downstairs,' Saul was going on. 'I won't be away long.'

She turned round to face him. 'I shan't be coming down again tonight,' she said. 'I really have got a headache.'

He gave her a worried look. 'You'd better take some tablets and get to bed, then, and have a good sleep. I'd like to get away early and get on the first possible flight to Paris. Then we can catch the TGV—you know—the high-speed train to Bordeaux—that'll be the quickest way.'

Of course! She remembered now. 'What makes you think I'm coming to France with you?' she said.

The dark eyes met hers with an enigmatic expression. 'Because I can't do without you,' he said. He went out and closed the door.

Nicola pulled up a chair to the open window. Behind the dark trees at the end of the tennis court the sun was beginning to set in a blaze of apricot and pale grey. Laying her head back, she watched the colours change, the sky gradually darken. She felt very tired and quite peaceful. Not worrying about anything any more, not trying to fight Saul. What was the point?

Presently she heard the sound of voices from the direction of the front drive, car doors slamming. The guests were leaving. Nicola thought with pleasure of the coincidence of meeting Sir Victor Wells, and how much she would enjoy hearing him talk about her father. She would get in touch with him later, when he returned from his tour. She could find out the name of his agent.

It was almost dark now and the air was blowing in, cool. Nicola stood up to close the window and draw the curtains. Then, below her on the lawn, she saw two figures walking slowly together. Ros had come home. In the arc of light from the drawing-room window there was no mistaking that silver-gold fall of her hair and the way she swayed her hips slightly as she walked. No mistaking Saul either; the tall figure in the light grey suit could be nobody else.

Holding on to the window-frame, looking down at their slow progress together, Nicola had a dull sense of certainty. There was something about the intimacy of the two figures, the way Ros lifted up her face and the way his head bent to hers to listen.

It was very quiet now, and Nicola suddenly realised that she was holding her breath, her throat tight. The two figures had stopped now, in front of the gap in the laurel hedge. They were just outside the arc of light from the house but she could see them clearly. It was like watching a film you'd seen before and knowing what would happen next. Ros's pale arms went up round Saul's neck and he lowered his head to kiss her.

Nicola let out her breath in a long sigh. She closed the window, drew the curtains tightly across and switched on the light in the room. The mystery was finally solved. Ros was what Saul wanted, what he'd planned to get, and Ros was what Eleanor had wanted for Saul. She herself was just an outsider, a means to an end.

Slowly, as if it were a heavy weight, she pulled the chair away from the window and sank back into it. She felt no sense of shock, only a dull ache somewhere behind her ribs.

At that moment Tubb knocked at the door and came in with tea on a tray, accompanied by a plate of sandwiches and two white tablets in an eggcup. Nicola stared at the tablets and could scarcely repress a weak giggle. This was getting to be a habit. 'Mr Saul said to take these for your headache, miss,' he said, putting the tray on the bedside table. 'He wouldn't disturb you tonight, but could you be ready to leave at half-six in the morning and you can have breakfast at Heathrow? He wanted to miss the worst of the traffic across London.'

Taken by surprise, all Nicola could do was to nod and ask Tubb if he would give her a call at six o'clock to make sure she was awake. He promised to do so, and added that he hoped her headache would soon be better. She thought his look was pitying. He must be wondering why a newly engaged young woman should have so many headaches and look so miserable most of the time. As if to cheer her up he said brightly, 'I've dealt with those clothes of yours, miss, that the wine got spilt on. I've got some special stuff for stains that works a treat. They'll come up fresh as a daisy.'

Nicola tried to look pleased. She wouldn't for the world hurt the little man's feelings by telling him that she would never wear that dress again.

When Tubb had gone Nicola drank the tea and ate a sandwich mechanically, trying to sort out her muddled thoughts, finally concluding that she would have to go to France with Saul tomorrow. If she refused he would find some way of making her change her mind—he always managed to do that. That was what love did for you. It undermined all your good resolutions and turned you into a zombie. Disgusted with her own feebleness, she consoled herself with the thought that it wouldn't last much longer. Only another week and it would all be over.

'I can't do without you,' he'd said. That could only mean that it was a business trip and that he needed her as a secretary. She knew that the Jarrett family had owned a vineyard in the Bordeaux district for many years. Wearily she rubbed her hand across her forehead. At least it would mean getting away from this house. Anything was better than staying here.

She got up and cleaned her teeth, slid into her night-dress and, after setting her alarm for five-thirty, she swallowed the two tablets and got into bed. Soon, exhausted by all that had happened in the day, she fell into a heavy sleep.

'I expect you're wondering,' Saul said as they sat over rolls and coffee next morning at Heathrow, 'why the sudden rush to Bordeaux.'

'Yes,' Nicola said crisply, breaking a small piece of a roll. 'Would you like to tell me, or is that a mystery too?'

He frowned. 'What's the matter, Nikki? You seem strange this morning. Is your headache really better?'

'I'm fine,' she said.

He continued to stare at her for a moment or two. Then he shrugged and went on, 'It's like this. For some time I've been suspicious that there's been some funny business going on between Bordeaux and London but I couldn't get any proof of anything. I asked Paul to keep his eyes open while he was over there and yesterday evening I had a phone call from him, at the small hotel in Bordeaux where he's staying. Quite by chance he overheard a telephone conversation between Forbes, the manager there, and our man at The Wharf in London which gave him all the proof he needed. Rather rashly Paul barged in and confronted Forbes, who, of course, denied everything. Paul went back to Bordeaux to get in touch with me but just before he got back to the hotel he was set upon by a couple of toughs—Forbes's men, no doubt, who intended to put the fear of God into him, and he was considerably messed about.'

'Oh!' gasped Nicola. 'Poor Paul—is he badly hurt?'

Saul slanted her a keen glance. 'He'll live,' he said briefly. 'He was well enough to talk to me. He was in bed, being looked after by the good lady who owns the hotel. He's rather a favourite with her. If I know Paul he's rather enjoying being a little hero.'

'What a horrid thing to say!' Nicola burst out indignantly. 'I think it was very brave of Paul to confront the manager like that.'

'Do you?' said Saul, as if he couldn't care less for her opinion. 'Well, we shall see when we get there.' He put down his coffee-mug and pushed back his chair. 'Are you ready?'

'Just a minute,' she said, and he sat down again.

'I take it,' Nicola said carefully, 'that you need me on this trip as a secretary, not as a fiancée, so may we consider our agreement cancelled, at least for the moment?'

His gaze was fixed over her head at the passing crowd outside the window of the coffee-shop. 'Because of Paul?' he said.

'Well—yes. Isn't it obvious?'

He wouldn't want to have to explain everything to Paul, would he?

Saul lowered his eyes slowly to hers. 'Now that I come to think about it, I suppose it is. So—you wish to give me my ring back?' The ironic smile that she hated touched his mouth.

'Please,' she said in a businesslike voice. She took the ring-box from her handbag, fitted the ring into it and pushed the box to him across the table. 'Thanks for the loan,' she added drily.

'Thank *you*, Nicola.' He stowed the box away in an inside pocket, with as much care as if it had been made of priceless diamonds. 'Now, shall we go?'

On the plane Saul buried himself in the papers from his briefcase, after having bought a couple of magazines for Nicola. His silence didn't bother her and she didn't even open the magazines. She had a great deal to ponder on herself. But later, when they joined the high-speed train that would take them to Bordeaux, she thrust her speculations aside as she marvelled at the speed and comfort with which this wonder of modern technology conveyed them across the countryside—so fast that nearby objects were a blur and only the distant view seemed to move along with the train. She would have liked to share her excitement with Saul, but one glance at his stern profile convinced her that the luxury of such travel was something he took for granted, so she kept silent.

Coming from the air-conditioned atmosphere of the train into the Bordeaux street was like walking into a hot oven. Nicola hadn't arrived at the Manor with any idea of travelling, and she had been rather at a loss to know what to wear for this journey. The best thing she could find was the navy blue shirtwaister dress she was wearing with a light summer jacket. While she waited for Saul to find a taxi she pulled off the white jacket and the sun was fierce on her head and arms. She must buy a shady hat to wear while she was here if this weather continued, she reminded herself.

In the taxi Saul pulled off his own jacket and glanced at her as she lay back, wilting. 'Feeling the heat?' he said, rousing himself from his silent preoccupation. 'It'll be cool in the hotel; it always is. It's a small family place in the old district of the city. The large modern hotels are mostly on the outskirts. It's run by a Monsieur and Madame Bonnet, who look after one very well, and the cooking is excellent. We always stay there when we come to Bordeaux. You know it?'

'Bordeaux? No. I've only been to France twice, when I was studying French on my business course, and never further south than Paris.'

She looked through the window, where heat shimmered on the weathered stone of fine old buildings, interspersed with more modern ones of every size and shape imaginable. 'Looks interesting,' she said.

'Oh, it is,' he agreed. 'Bordeaux is full of history. It was a flourishing city at the time of the Roman Empire, and there are even the remains of a Roman amphitheatre here. And of course it once belonged to the kings of England. Remember Richard of Bordeaux?' He went on thoughtfully, 'When I was learning the business I spent some time here and when I got tired of the smell of wine I poked around Bordeaux. But that was in the

days of my youth,' he added wryly, 'before the heavy
burden of Jarrett and Sons fell upon my shoulders. Now
the only relaxation I allow myself when I'm here is a
stroll along the quayside, which is always interesting.'

The taxi turned into a narrow side-street of tall, well-
tended old buildings and drew up in front of one that
was much smaller and older-looking than the rest. It had
a painted sign saying 'Hotel Bonnet' over the entrance
door.

Saul had been right. Inside the small square reception
area the air was blessedly cool and smelled faintly of
wax polish and roses. On a dark wood table with heavily
carved legs was a bowl of white roses. There was also a
large, bound book and a brass ship's bell with a wooden
handle. The floor was made up of stone flags and the
width of the windowsill suggested that the walls must be
at least two feet thick. Two upright chairs stood facing
the staircase.

Saul took out a pen and scribbled something in the
book, then picked up the bell and rang it energetically.

Almost immediately there was the sound of light footsteps hurrying down the polished, uncarpeted stairs and
then a tiny woman in a black dress appeared at the
bottom.

She beamed at Saul. 'You have arrived, Monsieur Saul.
How pleased I am to see you.' She greeted him like an
old family friend, reaching up to kiss him on both cheeks.

'And I you, *madame*,' Saul replied. 'I have you to
thank for looking after my poor cousin.' They spoke in
French but Nicola's knowledge of the language was quite
good enough to follow what they said.

'He has been waiting for you,' Madame said. 'He will
be so glad you have come.' She directed a questioning
glance towards Nicola.

Saul said, 'This is my secretary, *madame*, Mademoiselle Oldfield. Nicola, my very good friend Madame Bonnet.'

'*Bonjour, madame*,' Nicola said, holding out her hand.

'*Enchantée, mademoiselle*.' Madame shook hands, beaming. 'If *mademoiselle* would like to sit down and wait while I take Monsieur Saul up to see his cousin...'

'Oh, don't trouble to climb up again,' Saul put in. 'I can find my own way. It's our usual room?' He took the stairs two at a time and disappeared round the corner.

Nicola sat down on one of the upright chairs and Madame Bonnet enquired if she would like coffee while she waited. Adjusting herself quickly to her role of secretary, Nicola thanked her and said she would wait and see what Monsieur Jarrett's wishes were. Madame nodded again and left her.

Saul seemed to be away a long time, and Nicola was conscious of feeling slightly nervous. She hadn't seen the cousins together since the night of the party, when it had been apparent that there wasn't much good feeling between them. And Saul had spoken so contemptuously when he'd told her of the attack on Paul. It made her blood boil just to think of it. He really could be thoroughly nasty if he felt like it. She worried, too, about how she and Paul would meet again and if it would be horribly embarrassing after the way they had parted.

At last Saul came down the stairs, and Nicola got to her feet eagerly. 'How is he?'

He was frowning and her heart sank. Surely they hadn't been having a row, when Paul was hurt?

'He wants to see you,' Saul said shortly. 'No doubt he'll give you a run-down of his symptoms himself. Come along.'

Beast! she thought as she followed him upstairs.

On the second floor he opened a door and ushered Nicola in. 'Here you are, Paul,' he said. 'Here's your good angel come to smile upon you.'

Nicola hesitated. The room was large and rather dim and she couldn't, at first, make out anything in it because the curtains were pulled against the bright sunlight. But as her eyes adjusted she saw that there was a big bed in the middle of the room. She went nearer. 'Paul?' she said tentatively.

She saw him clearly now. He was sitting propped up against the pillows. His fair curly hair had been cut away on one side to make room for a large plaster which ran diagonally upwards from his ear. His left eye was swollen and closed, and ringed by lurid shades of purple and yellow. His cheek was puffy and crimson and he held his left arm hitched into the opening of his pyjama jacket.

Trying to grin, he winced with pain and Nicola's heart melted. It reminded her so vividly of the old Paul she'd known before that disastrous last evening—the Paul she'd worked with so happily, had laughed and shared jokes with. The Paul who had teased her and sent her out to buy presents for his current girlfriend.

He held out an arm and she ran across the room to him. 'Paul, darling—what have they done to you? Your poor face!' Her voice was choky with affection.

He took her hand and pulled her down towards him and she kissed his cheek and let her face rest gently against his.

'But it isn't anything really bad?' She touched the bedclothes lightly where they lay across his body. 'No broken limbs?'

'Nothing,' whispered Paul through swollen lips, 'that won't recover now you're here, my sweet. Thank goodness it is you and not my mama. I begged Saul to keep her out of this at all costs.'

He seemed to be taking her presence for granted and she wondered what Saul had told him. She straightened up and turned round. The door was closed. Saul had departed.

Nicola looked at Paul, raising her eyebrows enquiringly.

'He'll have gone back to the vineyard, to see what's going on at the château there. To take over where I left off. He told you about what happened?'

'Yes.' She felt a quick stab of fear, visualising Saul being attacked by thugs with iron bars. 'But—but isn't it dangerous to go alone? Shouldn't he take the police with him?'

Paul tried to grin. 'Oh, Saul can look after himself. He's much better at it than I've ever been. Now come and sit down and talk to me and tell me how you come to be here. You're working for Saul, he tells me.'

She pulled up a chair near to the bed. 'Yes, temporarily. He needed a secretary part-time and I needed a job.'

'You mean—you've given me up?'

'I'm afraid so, Paul.'

He grabbed her hand and held it tightly. 'Nicola, dear, I'm on my knees to you about what happened that night at the party. I behaved like an absolute clot and I'm truly sorry. Can you forgive me?'

'Of course,' Nicola said lightly. 'Don't think any more about it. I didn't. I never took you seriously for a moment.'

'You mean you wouldn't have married me?'

She laughed merrily. 'Good gracious, no. You're not a marrying man, are you, dear Paul? Any girl could see that.'

There was a long silence. Then he sighed deeply. 'Oh, dear!'

She had tried to joke, to set his mind at rest. But he seemed so disconsolate that she said, 'What's the matter? Have I said something wrong?'

'Oh, Nicola, I hope so. I really hope so.' Then he fixed his one good eye on her earnestly. 'You see, I've found the one and only girl for me and I want her to take me seriously.'

Her heart sank. Surely he wasn't going to start *that* all over again? But he wasn't looking at her now. He was staring up at the ceiling.

'Her name's Antoinette,' he said dreamily, 'and she's the most wonderful girl in the world.'

Nicola breathed easily again. 'Tell me about her,' she said, 'or does it hurt your mouth to talk?'

He didn't seem even to have heard that question. He talked on for over an hour about Antoinette—her beauty, her charm, her sense of humour, her intelligence. 'And,' he finished triumphantly, 'she's a wizard about wines. Her dad owns a big vineyard over at St Emilion and Antoinette's been running the place for him while he's been off work with a broken leg. She's been superb,' he said reverently.

He was silent for a while. Then he leaned forward towards Nicola. 'You know, if I could persuade Saul to give me the management of the château here and I had Antoinette beside me we could really make a go of it.' His mouth drooped. 'But Saul's never let me have much responsibility. He thinks I'm a lightweight and maybe I have been up to now. But when something like this happens——' he touched his cheek '—it makes you think. And I mean to show him,' he added fiercely.

'Good for you,' Nicola smiled.

'And if I could offer Antoinette *that*,' Paul went on, 'it might boost my chances with her—and with her dad.'

Nicola said, 'Have you known her long?'

'I've known the family for some time. We do business with them. Our wines make a good blend in some years. But Antoinette's been somehow just a nice girl—until, the other day, we looked at each other and suddenly I *knew*. You know how it happens. It hits you like a brick.'

'I know how it happens,' Nicola said quietly.

But Paul wasn't listening. 'And then, the other night, when I thought my number was up,' he went on, 'all I could think of was that I'd never told Antoinette. That she'd never know how much I loved her.' He looked as if he was going to cry.

'But you could tell her now,' Nicola said. 'Why don't I phone her and tell her what's happened and ask her to come and see you?'

'Oh, *no*!' He was horrified. 'I couldn't let her see me looking like a dog's dinner.'

'It wouldn't make any difference if she cares about you.'

'I simply couldn't,' he said again. 'You see, I don't really know if she cares for me and I can't risk it.'

'Well, then,' Nicola suggested briskly, 'why not write to her? You can tell her how you feel. You could say you had to be away for a few days and that would give her time to think it over and you'd phone her when you return. I seem to have heard that they like to be businesslike about these things in France.'

Paul's one good eye gleamed. 'Nicola, you're a marvel. Bless you. My briefcase is over there—hand it up to me, there's a dear.'

Amused and rather touched, she complied. She helped him to get out a writing pad and pen, but before he could begin Madame Bonnet came into the room, bearing a tray, which she deposited on Paul's knee. '*Déjeuner*,' she announced. She lifted the lid from a bowl of soup. 'That will do you good, *monsieur*,' she beamed. She fixed her keen black eyes on Nicola. 'Monsieur Jarrett said you would wait until he returns, *mademoiselle*.'

Nicola thanked her and Madame departed.

As well as the soup there was a glass of red wine on the tray, a roll broken into bite-size pieces, with morsels of cheese beside it, and a little dish of grapes. Madame knew how to tempt an invalid's appetite.

Paul eyed the tray with relish. 'Looks good and smells good.' He seemed to have recovered his spirits. 'But why does Saul want you to wait? Aren't you hungry?'

'Starving,' she admitted.

'He's a selfish oaf,' Paul grumbled. 'Here, have some of my soup.' He loaded the spoon and held it out to her.

Nicola sipped a little from the tip of the spoon and rolled her eyes with appreciation. They both giggled and it was like old times in the office, when they'd shared some silly joke.

There was a sound from behind and she looked round. Saul stood in the doorway. In the dim light she thought he looked angry. She jumped to her feet. 'Saul, you're back. We were getting worried about you going to the château alone after what happened to Paul.'

'Good of you,' he drawled, 'but quite unnecessary.' He came further into the room, looking pointedly at the spoon which Paul was still holding out rather foolishly.

Paul put the spoon down; he evidently hadn't noticed the undercurrent between the other two. As Saul came further into the room he pulled himself up in the bed, saying, 'What did you find at the château?'

Saul stood stiffly at the foot of the bed. 'Forbes has cleared out,' he said, 'after burning all the books and papers. There are the remains of a sizeable bonfire.

There's only old Jules left now, and a couple of girls in the office, looking slightly shell-shocked. I've sent the girls home on a week's leave. The next thing to do is to take stock so we know what's missing. I shall need your help there, Nicola,' he added, 'then I must get back to London and tackle the mess from that end.'

Paul put in quickly, 'There's something I should like to suggest to you, Saul——'

'For Pete's sake,' Saul cut in dismissively, 'can't you see I've got enough on my plate? You just stay put and get yourself better—then you may be of some use. Come along, Nicola, I've no time to waste.'

With an expressive shrug of her shoulders towards Paul, Nicola followed Saul out of the room.

CHAPTER TEN

NICOLA had to run down the polished wooden stairs to keep up with Saul. It would serve him right, she thought, if I fell and broke my leg and he had two invalids to think about. But she reached the reception hall safely and caught up with Saul at the front door. She grabbed his sleeve and said, 'If you want me to work this afternoon I shall have to have something to eat.'

He didn't stop or look round. He said, 'That's attended to. There's a hamper in the car. We can eat when we get there.'

He was driving Paul's green BMW. Nicola had often driven happily with Paul in this car and it wasn't a pleasant change to have Saul beside her instead, silent and grim. He didn't speak until they were out of the city with a long straight stretch of road ahead, then he slewed his eyes round briefly and said, 'Well, what did you think of our invalid?'

'He looks terrible,' she replied. 'I was quite shocked. And he did not give me a run-down of all his symptoms as you so nastily suggested he would.'

Now that she had to accept that her dream of love had been nothing more than a midsummer madness she had a sense of freedom. She could say anything to Saul and not care what he thought of her. 'I think you're beastly about Paul,' she said. 'Every time you speak to him or mention him you try to put him down. Do you dislike him?'

'I don't dislike him,' Saul said indifferently. 'I merely think he's rather a lightweight.'

A lightweight! That was what poor old Paul himself had said so ruefully.

'I should have thought,' Saul went on without taking his eyes from the road ahead, 'that you would agree with me. I seem to remember that "rabbit" was the word you used to describe Paul on that first occasion we met at the party.'

She flushed angrily. 'It's like you to bring that up. Anyway, it's all in the past now. This experience has changed him. I knew that as soon as we began to talk. He's much more serious.'

'Really?'

'Yes, really,' she said hotly.

The silence that followed was a snub in itself but she didn't care. She'd said what she wanted to say and she knew only too well how dangerous Saul could be if his temper was aroused. She shivered at the memory and in order to blot it out she reminded herself of what she knew about the vineyard and its winery.

She had never accompanied Paul on his trips abroad and had guessed that a secretary might cramp his style, but she'd been interested in the workings of the company, and had studied the large map of the Bordeaux wine-making region which hung on the wall in Paul's office. The Hautmont-Jarrett vineyard was marked with a ring.

Paul had told her, when she first came to work for him, that the vineyard had been bought from the Hautmont family by his great-grandfather, and the name had been retained, as was sometimes the custom. He had told her about the most exclusive vineyards with their great châteaux, where the most famous clarets in the world were produced at prices which made her head spin. The Hautmont-Jarrett vineyard, he had said, was one of the smaller ones. 'It boasts a château of its own,' he had told her, 'but it's really little more than a large country house. The manager lives in the château—lucky devil—I've always envied him that job myself, but I don't suppose Saul would consider me even if Forbes left. He's been there for years—my father engaged him when Dad was running the company after Saul's father died.'

Nicola remembered all this as they drove along. And now Forbes had decamped and Paul saw his chance to get his wish, if only he could persuade his cousin that he'd turned over a new leaf and was really in earnest. She wished she could help Paul, but she knew she would do more harm than good by interfering, so she put his troubles out of her mind and concentrated on the passing scenery.

It was very hot in the car but the breeze that blew in through the open windows and fanned her cheeks was cool as Saul drove—as usual—at speed. She guessed that they must be travelling roughly along the line of the Gironde estuary, which probably accounted for the flatness of the countryside around. She thought it was rather like East Anglia, only instead of cereal crops there were vines. Vines everywhere you looked, for miles around. They passed through one or two small villages and she saw a rather grand building which must, she thought, be one of the famous châteaux which Paul had told her about. She wished that Saul weren't driving so fast; she would have liked to have a good look at it. A few miles further on there was another château, but it was set back from the road, so that she saw even less of it.

Finally Saul did slow down to turn and she read the painted noticeboard on a gatepost which said 'Château Hautmont-Jarrett'. They were here.

The wide, rough drive was overhung by low trees. As the car turned a corner, the château was before her.

It was a long, two-storey building, with a terrace in front, and Nicola's first impression was of dazzling sunlight on the few patches of white plaster wall which were not smothered by rampant vines. There were blue-painted shutters to the windows, under a pink-tiled roof. They drove round the side of the building, passed under an archway in one of the two side-wings, and came to a halt on the cobblestones of a shady inner courtyard.

Saul jumped out of the car, pulled out the hamper, and opened the heavy oak back door of the château with a key. He led the way along a tiled passage into a large room overlooking the terrace beyond which rows of vines stretched out into the distance.

Nicola glanced round quickly. It was a graciously proportioned room, with solid dark wood furniture, some of it elaborately carved, and comfortable chintz-covered chairs and sofas. There was a haze of dust over everything and newspapers and cushions lay scattered on the marble floor, but there was nothing that an hour or two's work with soap and water and polish wouldn't put right. Nicola made a mental note to tackle the job if she got the opportunity. If Paul intended to show the château to Antoinette it must look inviting.

'It's too hot to eat in here,' she said. She threw open the French windows. 'Will you take a couple of chairs out, please, and we can picnic on the terrace?'

Saul was scowling and she thought at first that he was going to refuse. But he did as she asked and she carried out the hamper and put it down between them on a white-painted iron table, taking out plates, glasses and knives.

'I'll allow myself five minutes,' he said, opening a bottle of wine. He poured wine into the glasses, spread pâté on a large hunk of baguette and swallowed it, followed by another hunk. Then, tossing down a glass of wine, he got to his feet.

'I'll go and find Jules. He's the *maître de chai*—the cellar-master—and the only remaining member of the staff, apart from the two girls in the office, whom I've sent home. Poor Jules doesn't know what's going on and I want to reassure him. I'll come back and let you know when I'm ready for you.'

Nicola didn't have to persuade herself any longer that he regarded her as his secretary now. That, she told herself, made things easier.

She ate all the food she wanted and packed the remains back into the hamper. Then she went indoors and took a look round the château. There were three large rooms downstairs, one of which was being used as an office. Here she armed herself with a notebook and pen. Saul was not going to find fault with her as a secretary.

She climbed the imposing staircase to the first floor and found five bedrooms, one of which had obviously been vacated hastily. There were also two old-fashioned bathrooms with fittings which would have cost the earth at a London antiques market.

'Nicola!' Saul roared from the direction of the hall, and she hurried down to him.

'I've been taking a look round,' she said. 'Everything's as you'd expect but——' she sighed '—what a lovely house it is. It would make a delightful home if it were put to rights.'

He looked rather hard at her but made no reply. 'We'll get started,' he said, leading the way down to an immense cellar where the wine was stored in huge wooden tubs. Further on there were long racks filled with bottles. Nicola was introduced to Monsieur Jules, and duly shook hands. The *maître de chai* was a tall, stately man with white hair, wearing a long brown linen coat. He looked very worried and immediately began to fire questions, which Saul dealt with briefly. They moved from rack to rack, Saul dictating a bewildering mass of data to Nicola. It presented no difficulty to her; she was familiar with all the company's wines and very soon she had filled several pages with her lists.

'Is that all, Jules?' Saul said at last and Jules murmured,

'*Oui, monsieur,*' and shook his head gravely.

'I'll leave you, then,' Saul told him. 'I'll send you some help along as soon as I can manage it. Ready, Nicola?'

She closed her notebook and followed him out of the cellar.

Not a word was exchanged on the drive back to Bordeaux. Once there, Saul stopped the car outside the hotel and reached behind him for the picnic basket. He dumped it on Nicola's lap, saying, 'Will you take this in? I'm going to park Paul's car where I found it. I shan't be needing it again. There'll be a taxi around somewhere to get to the station.'

So he was leaving straight away, was he? And was she supposed to be going with him?

'Out you get,' he said. 'Time is of the essence.'

She tumbled out of the car with the basket and he slammed the door behind her and was off along the narrow road, driving French style—like a rocket.

There was nobody in the reception hall. Nicola put the basket down and went through into a small lounge, where she settled into a comfortable chair to await Saul's further instructions. A good secretary to the end, she thought, with a twist of her lip.

Saul was providing an excellent example of a tycoon in action. He flashed like a meteor across the sky. She herself was feeling like a spare part. She had no idea what she was expected to do. Saul's evident purpose was to get back to London as quickly as possible—to attend to the business crisis, or to see Ros? Both, probably.

She heard him come in, cross the hall and run up-stairs. When his step sounded again, coming down the stairs, she stood up and went to meet him.

'The doctor's been and Paul's much better,' he told her. 'I'll be on my way now. Thanks for your help, Nicola; it's been invaluable.' He tapped the pocket of his jacket, where he'd stuffed her notebook. 'You'll stay here with Paul, of course, until things are sorted out. I've booked a room for you.' He drew out a roll of notes. 'Here are some francs to keep you going. I know you haven't had an opportunity to draw any cash.'

As she seemed about to protest he said, 'No, you must take it.' He smiled crookedly. 'You're still on the company's payroll, you know. Buy yourself a hat; you should be wearing one down here. The sun's very fierce.'

He began to turn away, then seemed to remember something. 'When is Gran due home?'

Her head jerked back. 'Gran? Oh—oh, not for weeks yet—she's away for a month.'

He nodded. 'That gives us plenty of time to sort things out and arrange things before then. *Au revoir*, Nicola.' Then he was gone.

Nicola watched the door close behind him. If she could have run away somewhere and curled up like a wounded animal it might have helped. There was nothing to stop her—Saul had given her money, paid her off for her services, she thought bitterly. But something in her nature and upbringing made her refuse to run away. She went up to Paul's room and knocked at the door.

Paul was sitting in a chair beside the bed, wrapped in a dressing-gown. He looked much more cheerful than when she had last seen him.

'Pull up a chair, Nicola, and I'll tell you my good news.'

'Antoinette?'

He shook his head. 'No, not yet. You won't believe this, but Saul has actually asked me to go over to take charge of the vineyard just as soon as I can get about— which will be tomorrow. I know it's only because there's nobody else he can send at the moment, but——' he winked his one good eye '—once I've got a toe in the door he won't find it easy to get me out again.' He chuckled delightedly. 'How about that, then?'

'Congratulations,' Nicola said warmly. It looked as though *somebody's* dreams were going to come true.

Nicola ate a solitary dinner at a small table in the dining-room. The other diners were in parties of three or four and chattered away in a variety of languages but except for a smile or two in her direction nobody took any notice of her, which suited her very well. She wasn't in a holiday mood and her thoughts were concerned with how she could best get through the next few days until the inevitable break came with Saul. She wasn't even sure how it would happen. He had promised to make everything clear to her at the end of this week; she wondered if he remembered. He was so distracted by the company's crisis that she could hardly expect him to.

The next day was Tuesday. Nicola spent the morning browsing round the shops in the boulevards. She bought herself a shady straw hat, as Saul had directed, and enjoyed a small secret pleasure that he should have thought of her well-being. There was no sign of the heat abating so she also bought a couple of the thinnest sundresses she could find, in cheerful colours of red and yellow. She drank a long, deliciously cool drink at an open-air café and before returning to the hotel she couldn't resist buying a baguette and some delicious-looking cheese, and a bottle of fruit juice.

She was amazed on walking into the hall to see Paul sitting there fully dressed. 'It's no use, Nicola,' he blurted out. 'I just can't wait. I simply must get out to the château. I've written to Antoinette. We'll post it on the way. What've you got there—food? Oh, good, that means we needn't stop for lunch. Just toss the lot in the BMW and we'll get cracking.'

'Should you be driving?' Nicola asked as they went out to the car.

'Oh, yes, I'm fine. Just a bit stiff—it'll wear off.'

It was a good time to start, as most of Bordeaux seemed to be enjoying its siesta and the streets were fairly quiet. Within half an hour Paul was turning the car in at the entrance to the Hautmont-Jarrett vineyard. They went straight to the terrace, where Nicola sank into one of the chairs and poured herself a long drink from the bottle of fruit juice they had brought with them, while Paul limped around gloating over the château which was soon to be his home. His enthusiasm was infectious and when he came to sit beside her on the terrace they were both full of plans over lunch. Tomorrow, Nicola promised, she would start the cleaning-up process while Paul began to organise the office, ready for it to be functional again when the time came.

'I'll have to have a word with Jules about taking on some new staff. It seems that Forbes got rid of just about everyone, except his accomplices, before he left,' Paul said. 'It's a blessing that it's June,' he added; 'at least there's very little to do to the vines just now.'

He went on to explain how because of the depth of their roots the vines didn't need watering. In fact the more sunshine they received the better, and there was even a possibility that this year might turn out to be a special vintage. 'It'll be September when the fun starts. I wonder if the picking is done by machine here? I must ask Jules.'

It was only when Nicola told him how impressed she was with his knowledge that Paul admitted that he'd taken a course in viticulture when he first started to work in the firm. 'It's not done me much good up to now,' he confessed. 'But in the future . . .' He rubbed his hands expressively, his one good eye sparkling as he pulled himself to his feet and limped off in search of Jules.

While he was away Nicola explored the kitchen quarters at the end of a stone-flagged passage and made a mental note of everything that would be needed for what she thought of as the spring-cleaning. She was looking forward to it. Hard work, she told herself grimly, was the best antidote to a broken heart.

In the days that followed she found that that was partly true. There was so much to do that there was no time to sit and brood, and if her cheeks were once or twice damp with tears she could always blame the heat.

She and Paul spent every day at the château, returning to the hotel in the evening in time for dinner. Paul's appearance improved rapidly. The swelling went down and he could open his eye. The bruise-marks were disappearing fast and only the plaster remained to bear witness to the savagery of the attack.

Nicola wrote a long letter to Gran. 'Saul and I have come to Bordeaux on business,' she began, and then broke down in tears because everything was so utterly, utterly false and horrible and she felt so bad about lying to Gran. She contented herself, in the end, with describing Bordeaux, with its old buildings and river and the excellent shops, and then went on to talk about the vineyard and the château, and ended up by saying how she was looking forward to news of the family in Australia and to telling Gran about everything here when she came home again. Saul was well and wildly busy, she said, and could think of nothing more to say about him, which made her burst into tears again.

In short a pretty poor effort, she thought miserably as she wiped her eyes and swilled her face before preparing for bed, but the best she could do.

The nights, after she went up to the tiny room under the eaves which Madame had found for her, were the worst, of course, as nights always were when misery was eating deep into you. But sheer physical tiredness made sleep possible, and somehow she got through the dark hours and rose the next morning ready for work again.

The château was beginning to look cared for and welcoming. Paul would be able to invite Antoinette to visit him here without any qualms. On Thursday evening, after dinner, there was a phone call from Saul in London. 'He never tells you much,' Paul said to Nicola afterwards, 'but he sounded reasonably satisfied so we must hope for the best. He'll be coming back here but he didn't say when. That's about all I got out of him. I told him that we'd been out at the château every day and how marvellous you'd been in transforming it. He said he wasn't surprised. I think your stock's going up in the company, Nicola.' Nicola made no comment.

On Saturday morning Paul was up in the clouds. Over breakfast in the hotel he told Nicola that he had heard from Antoinette. 'She's had my letter and she wants me to go and see her as soon as I come back to Bordeaux. Of course, she thinks I've been away; that's what I told her when I wrote to her. Am I fit to be seen, do you think?' He stood up and examined his face in the gilt-framed mirror on the wall behind their table. 'You don't think she'll get a horrible fright and run away screaming?'

'Sit down and eat your breakfast,' Nicola urged. 'She'll think you look wonderful.'

He was in a shocking state of nerves. He couldn't eat a bite, he said, and only tossed down a small cup of coffee when Nicola insisted. He had to go and see Antoinette right away, he said. He couldn't live in this state of uncertainty. He would drop Nicola off at the château and then drive straight to St Emilion. 'Is that OK with you, Nicola?' he asked.

'Yes, yes,' she soothed. 'Bring Antoinette back with you to see her future home.'

Paul worried out loud all the way to the château. What did Nicola think? Would Antoinette have written like that if it hadn't been all right? She wouldn't ask him to go and see her if she intended simply to give him the brush-off, would she? She was such a straightforward, honest girl. She would want to tell him herself if she didn't care about him—she wouldn't just put it in a letter. He see-sawed between hope and despair. Nicola put in an encouraging, 'Yes, of course,' and, 'No, I'm sure she wouldn't,' now and again but she didn't think he heard her.

At the château he unlocked the door for Nicola. 'Wish me luck,' he said.

'Oh, I do—and you look fine.' He did indeed look very attractive, she thought, tall and slim in white trousers and pale blue shirt, his brown eyes very bright, the bruises almost unnoticeable.

'Bless you,' he said, squeezing her hand hard. Then he got back into the car and drove away.

Nicola watched the car disappear and then, turning back into the big, empty château, she felt loneliness settling round her. In the last few days she'd been too busy to think very much, but there was nothing left for her to do now. All the rooms were clean and tidy, ready for Antoinette to stamp her own individuality on them—if she wanted to, and somehow Nicola felt certain that she would.

Paul had been busy too, conferring with Jules about new staff, making himself familiar with the complicated machinery he had proudly shown her in the great sheds where the wine was made. He'd always been around, and his spirits had risen as the days had gone by and he'd begun to get the feeling of the place which he fully intended to manage from now on. They had filled up the fridge and Nicola had prepared snack meals. They had talked together and laughed and it had been pleasant and relaxing—like old times in London.

All that was finished now, she thought. There was nothing more for her to do, and she wasn't going to hang about to make a third with Paul and Antoinette. Saul had said he would come back and they would 'sort things out', but there wasn't anything to sort out now. The great mystery was explained. He had serious business worries, she knew that, and thought that that would account for his curtness, almost rudeness to her before he left. But his business worries had nothing to do with her. And anyway, he had Ros.

Suddenly the pain that she'd been holding back struck her and she hugged both arms round her middle, trying to push back the leaden feeling round her heart. She wouldn't let herself think of Saul—she *wouldn't*.

It felt stifling inside the house. There was a fan in the ceiling but she didn't know how to switch it on. She hunted round to find the switch, with no luck.

She was assailed by a frightening sense of unreality; the walls of the large room seemed to be closing in. Her yellow sundress was sticking to her and her forehead was wet when she passed a hand across it. She had to get out, she thought, panicking. She had to get outside. Picking up her big straw hat, she went out into the vineyard. The heat was scorching as she walked slowly between the rows of vines but her legs and feet were shaded and she had an illusion that she was walking waist-deep in a great sea of cool green water.

The only sound was from a tractor in the far distance, and the buzzing and whirring of insects near by. The sky above was a flat blue-white, and below her hands, among the green leafiness, fat bunches of little green grapes hung and seemed to swell by the minute in the sun they loved.

She felt a little dizzy. She mustn't stay out too long or she'd get heat-stroke, and that would put an end to the plan that was forming in her mind—the simple plan of leaving here tomorrow and making her way alone back to Watford.

It wouldn't be running away now. Her job was finished. Saul had helped her and she had helped him and now it was over. Fair enough.

At the end of a long row she turned back. Then a voice sounded from the distance. 'Nicola!' And again, 'Nicola!'

She eased the crown of her straw hat from her damp hair and pulled the brim further over her eyes, to peer towards the terrace. A single tall figure stood there. Not Paul, back so soon? That would be a bad sign.

But it wasn't Paul. Paul had been wearing light clothes and this figure was all dark.

Saul! It was like being struck by a great surge of high-voltage power. She stood quite still, her body quivering, until the wave passed over her and away. Then, summoning up all her strength, she began to walk towards him.

CHAPTER ELEVEN

SAUL came to meet her, walking between the long rows of vines. As he got nearer she saw that there was a look of pleasure on his face, and it was a small comfort that he should be pleased to see her. 'Hello, Saul,' she called out to him.

Then he stopped in front of her and the welcoming smile died on her lips. The look of pleasure had been merely a trick of the light. His expression was just as grim as when he'd left her at the hotel on Monday.

'What the hell are you doing out here at midday?' was his greeting. 'Do you want to get heat-stroke? And why aren't you wearing dark glasses? Come along in straight away.'

He turned and marched back towards the house.

Nicola glared after his retreating back. God, Saul could be unpleasant when he tried! But she had to admit that she felt uncomfortably hot so she followed him.

In the salon, Saul had already switched on the ceiling fan and drawn the curtains partway across the open windows. Nicola saw him clearly now. An air of utter weariness hung over him. His black hair was tousled and his eyes were heavy and shadowed. His grey and black striped shirt hung limply open and his black trousers had deep creases round the knees. He looked as if he hadn't been to bed for days.

They stood looking at each other in silence. Then Nicola broke into nervous chatter. 'Have you just ar-rived? It is terribly hot, isn't it? I'll get you a cool drink; there's some juice in the fridge. I'm afraid there's nothing stronger, unless you'd like to open a bottle of wine. Paul and I have just been snacking here this last week. Have you come to see Paul? I'm afraid he's not here just now. He went out...' Her voice trailed off and she looked away to avoid the dark, penetrating gaze fixed on her face.

'I came to see you,' Saul said.

Her head shot round. 'Me? Oh—oh, well, I'll just go and fetch a drink for us.'

In the kitchen she put two glasses and a bottle of fruit juice on a tray, aware that her hands were shaking. What was the matter with Saul? He seemed different—not angry exactly but different, and rather frightening.

She carried the tray back to the salon and found Saul pacing up and down, head bent, like an actor rehearsing his lines. She filled a glass and held it out to him.

He stopped pacing and took it. 'Thanks,' he muttered. He tossed off the drink and put down the glass. 'Sit down, Nicola,' he said. 'I want to talk to you.' He looked deadly serious.

She perched on the edge of a chair, holding her glass between her hands, looking down into it. So it was coming at last, then—the 'thanks very much and goodbye' she'd been expecting. Now that the time had come she felt quite calm, her emotions under control. She lifted her chin slightly. 'Yes?' she queried.

He sat down in the chair opposite, leaning forward slightly. He said, 'I've been driving all night and most of the time I've spent trying to think how to explain all this to you. Would it help if I began by thanking you sincerely for the way you've backed me up, and by telling you that our plan has succeeded brilliantly?'

He didn't seem to know what to say next. He sat with his hands clasped tightly before him, staring down at them.

Nicola drew in a breath. 'You don't have to explain anything,' she said. 'I know what it's all about.'

He looked up. 'You know? How can you know? Who told you?'

'Ros told me,' she said. 'But by then I'd almost worked it out for myself.'

The dark eyes narrowed. 'What exactly did Ros tell you?'

'That you two had always been in love—that her marriage had been a mistake—that now she was free you'd staged our engagement to lure her back and wasn't it time I removed myself from the scene so that you could get married.'

'Oh, God!' he exclaimed. He lay back, raising his eyes to the ceiling. Then, looking back at her, he asked, 'And you believed all that rubbish?'

'I saw you kissing her in the garden, the night before we left for France. That seemed fairly conclusive.'

'I wasn't kissing her, she was kissing me goodbye. She knows damned well I'd never marry her,' he went on, angry now. 'And anyway, she's after much bigger game than me. She wanted to tell me she was off to Greece the next day, to catch up with a shipping tycoon she'd met on the plane coming over. Satisfied?' he demanded fiercely.

She shook her head, bewildered. 'Then why did she say all those things to me?'

His mouth twisted contemptuously. 'At her mother's request, no doubt. It was Eleanor who wanted to get rid of you.'

She was more in the dark than ever but she felt suddenly lighter, as if a heavy weight had begun to lift from around her heart. Saul wasn't going to marry Ros—he was free. That didn't mean that he would fall in love with *her* of course, but still... She felt quite weak with relief.

Saul said, 'Listen, Nicola, and I'll explain.'

He was speaking quickly now and she tried to concentrate. It was all about Jarrett and Sons, and how the firm had been going steadily downhill since his father died, when his uncle, Paul's father, was running things.

'I wasn't long out of university myself,' he went on, 'and I had to learn the business. I was travelling a good deal and I didn't realise at first what was going on. My uncle had what is known as an alcohol problem, which means that he was rapidly drinking himself to death, and letting things slide. He was completely duped by Forbes and he made the ghastly mistake of putting him in charge of the vineyard here. Unknown to my uncle, Forbes and our man at The Wharf in London worked out a clever little scheme between themselves, which was taking hundreds of thousands of pounds out of profits every year. When my uncle finally died, and I had to take over, I found things in a pretty bad way. I've spent the last six years trying to put everything into shape but it's been against the odds. With one thing and another the life blood of the company has been draining away. One of my worst problems was Eleanor.'

Nicola blinked. 'Eleanor?'

He nodded tensely. 'When you and I met, things were reaching crisis point. The bank was getting awkward and I had to find more capital to put into the firm. The only way I could think of was by selling the Manor. It was much too big for us and I've never liked the house anyway. But I couldn't do it while Eleanor was there. I won't bore you by going into all the legal matters—wills and trusts and so on that have accumulated down the generations. The fact was that, as my uncle's widow, Eleanor was entitled to live in the house, enjoying the lifestyle she was accustomed to, unless she married again.' He laughed mirthlessly. 'As you may have noticed, Eleanor has been accustomed to an extremely lavish life-style—dinners, parties, clothes, servants, Rolls-Royce, chauffeur . . . all the things she demanded when my uncle was using the company's profits to please her and keep her quiet. My only hope was that she'd decide to marry Colonel Warwick—he's wanted her for years; God knows why.' He sank into his chair again, running a hand through his black hair. 'It seemed hopeless. She was too fond of being the lady of the Manor and queening it over local society.'

He stood up again and began to pace backwards and forwards. 'The maddening thing was that I'd got a buyer lined up for the Manor—a man I know who runs a very successful boys' prep school. He's wanted the Manor for ages and he offered to pay what the valuers decided. An infusion of upwards of a million pounds into the firm's capital was just what it needed.'

He sat down again, fixing his eyes on Nicola's face as if willing her to understand. 'Then we met and I think you can guess what happened next. I'd promised your gran to look after you while she was away, which meant taking you home with me. That was when I had the brainwave of faking our engagement. I knew that Eleanor would never play second fiddle to my wife, to a new mistress of the house, and that she might prefer to play first fiddle in the Colonel's establishment, although it was rather smaller. The night of her party, when I announced that our marriage was imminent, she knew she'd lost the game. She and the Colonel are going to be married in about six weeks. She's started packing already.'

Nicola was trying hard to follow all this. 'But what about her father? He's rather a dear.'

'Oh, Toby's going with her. The Colonel's quite happy to have him. They play chess together, and get along very well. And Toby gives Eleanor an addition to her dress allowance. The contract for sale is already being prepared by the solicitors, so——' he spread out his hands, smiling wryly '—that's the solution to what you called the mystery.' He leaned forward and looked deeply into her eyes. 'Are you disgusted with me, Nicola? I was afraid you might be if I told you about my devious scheme. I couldn't stop it once it had started, and you played up marvellously.'

She thought for some time before she replied, aware that he was watching her anxiously. At last she said, 'No, I'm not disgusted at all. I understand how it happened. I know how much your company means to you, Saul. You must be very happy.'

He looked vaguely surprised. 'Happy? Oh, yes, I am, of course.' But the happiness was muted and she felt that he must be very tired indeed.

She said, 'If you've been driving all night, why don't you go upstairs and have a sleep until Paul comes back? I know he's longing to talk to you. He's very keen. He's got all sorts of ideas for this place.'

'Oh, yes?' He yawned. 'I think I'll take your advice. A kip certainly wouldn't come amiss.'

He stopped on his way to the door. 'Oh, by the way, this letter came to the Manor for you.' He took a rather crumpled envelope from his pocket and handed it to her.

'From Gran,' Nicola said, taking it. 'That's nice. Thank you for bringing it.'

He went into the hall and she ran after him. 'It's the end room on the left.' She pointed upwards. 'I've made up the bed there.'

'Thanks.' With one foot on the bottom stair, he turned his head and gave her a weary smile. 'Making yourself at home already?' he said, and went slowly upstairs.

She stood still. What did that mean? He couldn't think she was angling to get Paul back, could he? No, of course he couldn't—it was just one of his nasty ironic remarks. She returned to the salon, poured herself another glass of fruit juice and settled down to read Gran's letter. Halfway down the first page she read:

My dearest girl, I have some rather disturbing news to tell you. Little Jeremy—the younger of the twins—appears to have some problem connected with his muscular development. His poor mother is very upset, as it apparently means quite a long period of treatment for him and he will need one person's almost constant attention to take him to hospital and to supervise his physiotherapy etc. This is obviously something I can help with and I've offered to stay on here as long as I'm needed. Roger is applying for a special permit for me, or something. I know you'll understand and approve and now you have Saul you won't miss your old gran too much. My greatest regret is that I won't be able to be at your wedding, if it is to be soon—which I'm sure it will.

There was a great deal more and Nicola read the letter through to the end. How like Gran to step in when she felt she could help, but—oh, goodness!—this meant that the fiction of the engagement would have to be kept up for months, possibly longer, while all the time it would be over and Saul would have gone out of her life. She read the letter through again and then sat for a long time, trying not to feel sorry for herself because she was going to be deprived of Gran's consoling presence when she would most need it, and then accusing herself of the worst kind of selfishness. Of course she would get along on her own perfectly well, wouldn't she? She wasn't going to let Saul Jarrett ruin her life.

She had just reached this rather unsatisfying conclusion when she was aroused by the sound of a car pulling up in the courtyard behind the château. Paul must have come back.

She ran along the passage and threw open the back door. Paul was helping a girl out of his car, a pretty, dark, slender girl in a white dress splashed with huge red poppies. Nicola knew immediately from the way he leaned towards her and touched her arm that this was Antoinette and that all was well.

He looked up and saw Nicola standing there. 'Hi!' He lifted an arm in salute and there was triumph in his voice.

She ran across the courtyard to join them. Paul was so excited that he made a hash of the introductions, but the two girls smiled at each other and kissed, and Antoinette said in excellent English that she was so happy to meet Nicola of whom she had heard so much. At the same moment Nicola was returning the compliment in almost the same words. They all laughed and the ice was broken.

Paul put an arm round each girl and led them into the salon. He said, 'Saul's here, isn't he? That's his car at the back.'

Nicola nodded. 'He turned up some time ago. He'd been driving all night and he was tired out. I sent him upstairs to have a sleep.'

'I'll go and wake him up,' Paul said. 'He's got to come and meet Antoinette. I won't be long.' They heard him clump away up the stairs.

Left alone with the French girl, Nicola knew immediately that she was going to like her. She seemed a trifle overcome by all that was happening, but she had poise and charm and there was warmth and humour in the dark brown eyes. The two of them sat down and took the first tentative steps towards friendship.

But while she was answering Antoinette's eager questions about the château a doubt was nagging at the back of Nicola's mind as she remembered how Saul had behaved at the hotel. Surely he wouldn't spoil everything now by being beastly to his young cousin?

When she heard Paul's footsteps coming downstairs alone her heart sank a little. But after a minute or two he appeared in the doorway, holding Saul's travelling bag, and she was reassured by the grin on his face.

'I've managed to wake the old ruffian up,' he said. 'I'm taking his gear to him. He insists on making himself pretty before he comes down to meet my fiancée.' He blew Antoinette a kiss and disappeared upstairs with the bag.

When he rejoined the two girls he said, 'Saul's having a cold plunge to wake himself up. He'll be among us again shortly.' He linked his arm with Antoinette's. 'Would you like to see the office, darling? It's pretty basic but I've got plans for it.'

It seemed to take Paul a considerable time to show Antoinette the office and when they came back into the salon her cheeks were very pink. Then Saul strode into the room.

Sleep had certainly revived him; he looked a new man. He had changed into khaki trousers and a lightweight khaki shirt. The sleeves were rolled up to disclose muscular forearms. He had shaved and brushed his hair and his black eyes were brilliant. Nicola thought he looked fabulous.

He went straight across to Antoinette and kissed her on both cheeks. They were evidently not strangers. 'This is splendid news, my dear,' he said, speaking in French. 'Welcome to the family Jarrett.' Then he added in English, 'Do you think you'll be able to keep my wayward young cousin in order?' He threw a laughing glance towards Paul and Nicola knew it was going to be all right. She let out a huge sigh of relief and then looked up quickly in case Saul had heard. But he wasn't taking the slightest notice of her. His attention was on the French girl, who dimpled, and said she thought she would be able to manage Paul.

Paul hugged her, said he was her willing slave and didn't they think it would be a good idea to open a bottle of Hautmont-Jarrett vintage to mark the occasion?

The next hour slid by with incredible speed. There was so much to talk about, so many plans to make. Antoinette was eager to see everything and they all trooped round the château as well as the vast cellars where all the work was done and the wine was stored.

Here Antoinette's bubbling gaiety changed to a look of professional gravity as she was presented to the *maître de chai*, Monsieur Jules, whose customary chilly politeness relaxed into something like warmth as he learned that Antoinette was connected with one of the top establishments in St Emilion. And when she began to ask him what were obviously intelligent questions about soil and grape varieties and methods of working, he was won over completely. Antoinette was admitted to the charmed circle—she was 'one of us'.

Monsieur Jules proudly showed off his beautifully kept stainless-steel equipment, the huge containers into which the grapes would be fed when the vintage came, to be crushed and pressed and put through all the carefully calculated processes until they finally ended up in bottles of Hautmont-Jarrett wine on the dining-tables of those favoured individuals who could afford them.

Nicola trailed around behind the party of experts and felt very much 'not one of us'. Saul, as owner, was being deferred to, of course, and he took no notice whatever of her, and when the tour ended with Monsieur Jules drawing samples of wine from a great oak barrel and handing them round to be tasted she begged to be excused, saying that she had had a cold and had no taste at all.

She was thankful when they said goodbye to Monsieur Jules and were out in the sunlight again. It was decided to leave Antoinette's inspection of the heavy machines in the outbuildings for another day, as it was time for the newly engaged couple to leave. Her mother was preparing a very special meal, Antoinette explained, and was inviting members of the family to meet Paul.

'We should be delighted if you would join us,' she added to Saul, 'and Nicola too, of course.' She smiled at Nicola, whom she had accepted as Saul's secretary.

Saul refused courteously, explaining that they had to return to London tomorrow, and there were several things here to be attended to first. Antoinette smiled prettily. 'Another time, then,' she said, bidding them *au revoir* and shaking hands before she climbed into Paul's car.

Paul opened the door on the driving side. 'See you both tonight at the hotel, then.'

Saul put an arm deliberately round Nicola's shoulder and drew her against him. 'Possibly,' he drawled.

Paul's look of blank surprise was comical. He goggled at Saul, then at Nicola and back again. 'Oh—oh, I see. Well, so long, then.'

He almost fell into the car, switched on the engine and reversed jerkily.

As the car passed through the archway, Antoinette's hand waved through the window. Nicola waved back and went on waving, although the car was out of sight. Now that she and Saul were alone again she felt almost sick with nerves.

His hand dropped from her shoulder immediately. He moved away, and in spite of the heat Nicola felt a cold chill. She couldn't think why Saul had chosen to give his cousin the obvious impression. But then she wasn't thinking clearly about anything just now.

They walked in silence through the back entrance door, along the tiled passage and into the salon, where Saul stood looking out of the window while Nicola moved about nervously, straightening cushions, gathering the wine glasses together. The silence was oppressive. She swallowed and said, 'Antoinette's lovely, don't you think? She's so pretty and so clever about wine. Paul's very lucky.'

Saul rounded on her and took the tray out of her hands, depositing it with a thump on the table again. He looked furiously angry and a spasm of fear tightened her stomach.

He took her by the shoulders and shook her none too gently. 'Why did you do it?' he shouted. 'Why did you let me think it was you?'

She wriggled away from him and sank on to the sofa as her knees buckled under her. Her mouth felt like sawdust and her palms were clammy. 'I—I don't know what you mean,' she faltered.

He stood before her, glaring down accusingly. 'You damn well do know. Ever since you handed me back the ring at Heathrow you made it clear that you wanted to get together with Paul again. And when we got here it seemed to me that he had the same idea.'

'You're imagining things——' she began helplessly.

'Everything pointed to it,' he cut in. 'You left me in no doubt at all. I told myself I should be pleased for the two of you. But when I got back to London I stopped fooling myself. I had a million things to do but all I could think of was you and Paul here together and I wanted to come back and wring his neck.' He thrust his hands into his pockets and turned away. 'Oh, Nikki, how could you do that to me?' he groaned. 'Were you trying to pay me back for the way I'd treated you?'

She sat lacing her fingers together. 'Of course I wasn't,' she said miserably. 'I really don't know what all this is about.'

He came back and sank down on the sofa beside her. 'That's been the trouble all along,' he said. 'I suppose it's all been my fault. We've both been stumbling around in the dark. Suppose we throw some light on the situation now?'

He took both her hands in his, and what she saw in his dark eyes made her tremble. 'I love you, Nikki,' he said very slowly. 'Will you marry me?'

A sob escaped her. 'Yes,' she cried. 'Oh, yes.'

Then his arms were around her and his mouth was on hers. It was a fiercely possessive kiss and it went on and on until she could hardly breathe. 'Darling, darling Nikki,' he said hoarsely at last. 'You pushed me away once because we weren't engaged. Would I get a different answer now that we are?'

The dark blue eyes raised to his were serious. 'It wasn't because we weren't engaged. It was because I was afraid.'

'Afraid? Of me?'

'Afraid of what you would think of me if I said yes. You see, that night of the party you suspected me of all sorts of horrid things and I thought that if I went to bed with you you might think I was trying to trick you or—or something.'

Saul groaned. 'What a cynical bastard I was turning into. My mother walked out on us when I was ten, and

I expect that's when the rot set in. And, you see, I'd never met a girl like you before.'

'I think you must have been looking in the wrong places,' Nicola said with a teasing smile.

'Don't make excuses for my rotten nature,' he said. 'Can you put up with me?'

She didn't need to reply. She reached up and laid her mouth on his and felt a shudder pass through him.

He stood up and yanked her to her feet triumphantly. 'We've got a whole château to ourselves,' he said. 'That bed upstairs is very comfortable.'

Arms entwined, they climbed the wide staircase. The ceiling fan was keeping the large bedroom deliciously cool. Saul pushed the door to with his foot and then his lips were hungrily pressed to hers and she felt round her back for the zip of her sundress. A moment later it was lying in a yellow heap on the floor. 'I don't think we'll need that either.' The final froth of white lace was removed and she sat on the bed while he took off her white sandals, kissing her toes one by one while she wriggled with delight.

He gazed up at her, white teeth gleaming against his brown cheeks. 'You're so very beautiful, my darling,' he said. 'You know I'd never do anything to hurt you, don't you? You trust me?'

'With my life,' Nicola said simply.

A moment later his own clothes had joined hers on the floor and they were lying together on the bed.

Saul made love to her with gentleness and passion, his hands and mouth exploring her body, finding sensitive places she'd never known about, stroking, caressing, as he murmured endearments. She knew he was holding back, controlling himself, giving her time. She didn't need time—she'd dreamed of this so often. 'Don't wait,' she cried out frantically at last. 'Please don't wait.'

It seemed like a high wave approaching. As he moved on to her she was borne up—up—until they were together on the crest and the wave was breaking. Nicola's head was thrown back as she bit into her lower lip, uttering little moans of pleasure, wanting this wonderful sensation to stretch on forever. But too soon it was over and they lay breathing hard, their hearts pounding against each other, their bodies clinging damply together.

Nicola shivered and Saul moved away to draw the coverlet over both of them. He touched her cheek with one finger. 'You're crying, my darling,' he said anxiously. 'Why?'

She buried her face in his shoulder. 'Because it was so wonderful,' she told him in an awed voice. 'I never knew it could be like that.'

He kissed her wet cheek. 'It was a revelation for me,' he said in a deep voice. 'After being celibate for so long and then—this. You just don't know——' His voice broke.

They slept and wakened and made love again and this time it was slower, deeper, infinitely satisfying. When it was over Nicola lay awake, staring up at the fan turning slowly on the ceiling. 'It seems terribly unromantic at a time like this,' she said, 'but I'm starving with hunger.'

Saul said, 'I've had three Mars bars and an apple since five o'clock this morning. What's on the menu?'

Nicola glanced towards the window; outside it was almost dark. 'Aren't we going back to the hotel, then?'

Saul stretched luxuriously, arms above his head. 'We are not. I like it here. We're going to stay.'

'But we can't.' Nicola sat up in bed. 'I've got nothing here except the dress I came in this morning.' She indicated the crumpled heap of yellow on the floor.

'That's simple,' Saul told her. 'Your bag from the Manor's in the back of my car. You packed it the night before we left. I didn't think you'd want to go back there so I brought it with me. So—any more problems?'

'What are we going to eat?' she said. 'There's nothing much in the fridge. Only eggs and cheese and mushrooms. And there's a loaf of bread I brought this morning—and lots of fruit.'

'Fair enough,' Saul told her. 'I remember you whipped up a very tasty omelette for me once before. The night we got engaged, remember?'

She wrinkled her nose. 'Oh, don't remind me of that.'

'OK,' he said, 'but it does remind me of something.' He heaved himself up in the bed and reached down to the floor to extract a familiar ring-box from his trouser pocket. 'I've been carrying this around as a hostage to fortune,' he said and, taking out the ring, he slipped it on Nicola's finger. 'There,' he said. 'That's better.'

She switched on the bedside lamp and held up her hand to admire the glitter of diamonds. 'Much better,' she sighed. 'I've missed it. I've grown fond of it and I really don't care that it's artificial. I'm sure you can't afford real diamonds just now when there are all these money problems.'

He chuckled. 'What a prudent little wife I'm going to have—but we're not quite broke, you know. Darling Nikki,' he laughed, 'you don't think I'd buy a girl like you an artificial ring, do you? I knew by then that you weren't an artificial kind of girl.'

She gasped. 'You mean I've been wearing a valuable ring all this time?'

'It suits you,' he said complacently.

It took a little while for her to get her breath back, and of course she had to thank him properly, but at last she slipped out of bed and made for the bathroom. As she passed round Saul's side of the bed his arm shot out and grabbed her round the waist. 'You've got a dear little mole on your left hip,' he said, drawing her closer. 'Perhaps I'm not so hungry after all,' he mused.

She wriggled away. 'Well, I am,' she said, 'and when I get back I expect to find my bag waiting for me.' She bent and kissed the tip of his nose.

'OK, you win,' he grumbled, letting her go.

But as she reached the door she heard him mutter darkly, 'This time.'

CHAPTER TWELVE

WHEN she returned to the bedroom Nicola found her travel bag waiting for her and she could hear Saul splashing about in the second bathroom. She rummaged through the bag and found a thin, ice-blue shift, just the thing for a warm evening. She slipped it on, coiled her hair into a chignon, applied a little more shadow and mascara to her eyes and went down to set the small table in the salon.

Saul came down as she was whipping up the eggs for the omelettes. He leaned against the kitchen door-post, watching her and telling her every thirty seconds how remarkably beautiful she was. He had changed too and was wearing white trousers and a white silk shirt and she had to keep her eyes very firmly upon the omelette-pan.

When the omelettes were ready they carried them to the table. Saul opened a bottle of wine and poured a little into Nicola's glass. She waved the glass backwards and forwards under her nose, sniffing consideringly. Then she took a sip and raised her eyes. 'Ah! A spirited little wine!' she said with due appreciation.

Saul chuckled delightedly. 'You're getting the idea.' He slanted her a wicked glance. 'I'm so glad your cold's quite better.'

'Oh, that! That was because of Monsieur Jules. I was terrified of making a fool of myself when you were all being so beastly knowing. Monsieur Jules is rather—er— *formidable.*' She gave the word its French pronunciation. 'But he knows you're the Big Boss, the one-who-must-be-obeyed, so he defers to you.' She smiled up at him under her long lashes as she added, 'Just as I do.'

'Careful,' Saul said darkly. 'I'm beginning to get ideas. If you want to have any dinner you'd better get on with it.'

Nicola pulled a face at him and picked up her knife and fork.

Never had omelettes looked so delicately golden or tasted so good. Never had bread been so crisp or peaches so luscious. Nicola cooked a second omelette for Saul and helped him to finish the bottle of wine. Their conversation didn't make a lot of sense but they laughed a lot and touched each other's hands frequently. They finished up everything on the table, leaving only the end of the long loaf which they kept for breakfast. Then they moved to the comfort of the sofa, with the coffee-tray on a low table beside them. Nicola curled up against Saul and felt a little tipsy and blissfully happy.

He took a long drink of black coffee, then shook his head as if he was awakening from a dream. 'I suppose we'd better start making plans, little girl,' he said.

'Hmm?' She snuggled closer, eyes closed.

'Plans,' he repeated, 'for our wedding.'

That wakened Nicola up. She opened her eyes and sat up. 'Oh, yes, let's,' she agreed.

'We'll get married just as soon as Gran comes back,' Saul said.

Nicola pulled herself together. 'Oh—oh, yes, I forgot.' She took Gran's letter from her handbag and handed it to Saul. He read it through carefully and put it down on the table.

'How like Gran,' he said.

Nicola agreed. Then she said, 'But I was quite devastated when I thought that I'd have to go on for months trying to pretend to be blissfully happy when all the time I was utterly miserable.'

'Never again, my darling, so long as I can help it.' He drew her closer again and kissed her tenderly. Then, 'This alters things,' he said. He closed his eyes for a few moments, thinking. Then he said, 'We'll get married next Wednesday. We'll just steal away by ourselves and then leave for a couple of nights in Paris. From there we can fly on to Australia to spend the rest of our honeymoon.'

She stretched out her left arm and pinched it between the finger and thumb of her right hand. 'I'm not dreaming,' she said.

He leaned over and kissed the place on her arm, which was turning pink, and then his lips moved up slowly to hers. 'You're certainly not dreaming—does that prove it?'

'Yes,' she said. Then her practical self popped up its head. 'But—can you spare the time?'

'Oh, yes, I think so. I'll hand things over to my second-in-command in London. He'll hold the fort while I'm away. I think we both deserve a break before we come back to tackle all the things that will need to be done. I'll be up to my ears at the office and we'll have to arrange the move from the Manor—when Eleanor has taken what she wants. And there's Gran's house in Watford. We must find someone to keep an eye on that while she's away.'

Nicola nodded slowly. 'You know, I shouldn't be at all surprised if they want to keep her with them out there. A great-grandmother is a handy thing to have around— especially a great-grandmother like Gran. I think she might be happy there, with all those people needing her. But I should miss her. We've been together so long.'

A shadow passed across her face and Saul stood up and held out a hand. 'Let's go out and look at the stars,' he said.

The air was warm and there was a smell of earth and growing things. It was very still—just the hum of insects and the flap of wings as a bird rose from somewhere near them out of the leaves, squawking its displeasure at being disturbed. There was no moon but the sky was encrusted with stars, huge and incredibly bright—so bright that they cast a silvery haze across the vines.

Nicola let her hand trail over the leaves as she strolled along beside Saul, her head against his shoulder. 'It's lovely here,' she sighed. 'I could almost envy Paul and Antoinette, living in a place like this.'

Saul was silent for a time and then he said, 'I could offer you somewhere almost as good. How would you feel about making our home at Hill Cottage?'

Nicola stopped dead. 'You mean that cottage where we had lunch with your friends—the cottage that had a fantastic view of the South Downs?'

'That's the one,' Saul said. 'I've got an option on the purchase. I arranged it on the day we lunched there, when you said you thought the place was heaven. I had an idea it would be heaven living there with you. It was another hostage to fortune, like the ring. What do you think? I've got to let them know by tomorrow.'

'It would be perfect,' Nicola said. 'But wouldn't it be too far from London for you?'

'Reasonable commuting distance—and we'd have a small flat in town as well.' He began to plan. 'We'll install Tubb and Bo'sun at the cottage. There's a good pub in the village with a dartboard, and we can take Bo'sun's favourite chair with us.'

Nicola began to laugh weakly. 'I feel like a little girl again, opening my Christmas stocking. All these lovely surprises!'

He put a hand on either side of her face and raised it to the stars. 'I love you, Nikki,' he said, his voice deep. 'I can't get along without you. I want to give you everything.'

She linked her arms round his neck and reached up to kiss him. 'Darling, darling Saul—you've given me so much. I can't think of anything more you could give me.'

'Can't you?' he said. 'I can.' His hand moved up from her waist and closed over her breast.

No more mystery. She knew exactly what he meant and she shivered with the anticipation of delight as they walked together, hand in hand, back to the château.

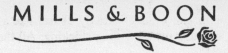

MILLS & BOON

OCTOBER 1994 HARDBACK TITLES

Romance

Lovers Not Friends *Helen Brooks*	H4148	0 263 14109 8
A Very Stylish Affair *Emma Darcy*	H4149	0 263 14110 1
Element of Risk *Robyn Donald*	H4150	0 263 14111 X
Between Two Loves *Rosemary Hammond*	H4151	0 263 14112 8
Love, Desire and You *Rosalie Henaghan*	H4152	0 263 14113 6
Step in the Dark *Marjorie Lewty*	H4153	0 263 14114 4
Innocent Deceiver *Lilian Peake*	H4154	0 263 14115 2
A Passionate Deceit *Kate Proctor*	H4155	0 263 14116 0
Whisper of Scandal *Kathryn Ross*	H4156	0 263 14117 9
Lovestorm *Jennifer Taylor*	H4157	0 263 14118 7
Calypso's Enchantment *Kate Walker*	H4158	0 263 14119 5
To Have and To Hold *Sally Wentworth*	H4159	0 263 14120 9
Saving the Devil *Sophie Weston*	H4160	0 263 14121 7
Dream Man *Quinn Wilder*	H4161	0 263 14122 5
Burden of Innocence *Patricia Wilson*	H4162	0 263 14123 3
Threads of Destiny *Sara Wood*	H4163	0 263 14124 1

LEGACY *of* LOVE

The Astrologer's Daughter *Paula Marshall*	M345	0 263 14161 6
Friday Dreaming *Elizabeth Bailey*	M346	0 263 14162 4

LOVE ON CALL

Heart on the Line *Jean Evans*	D263	0 263 14167 5
A Different Destiny *Meredith Webber*	D264	0 263 14168 3

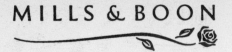

MILLS & BOON

OCTOBER 1994 LARGE PRINT TITLES

Romance

Apollo's Legend *Rosalie Ash*	751	0 263 13927 1
Enemy Within *Amanda Browning*	752	0 263 13928 X
The Colour of Midnight *Robyn Donald*	753	0 263 13929 8
Summer of the Storm *Catherine George*	754	0 263 13930 1
A Perfect Seduction *Joanna Mansell*	755	0 263 13931 X
Outback Temptation *Valerie Parv*	756	0 263 13932 8
Divided by Love *Kathryn Ross*	757	0 263 13933 6
Ice at Heart *Sophie Weston*	758	0 263 13934 4

LEGACY *of* LOVE

Beau's Stratagem *Louisa Gray*	0 263 14016 4
Escape to Destiny *Sarah Westleigh*	0 263 14017 2

LOVE ON CALL

No Shadow of Doubt *Abigail Gordon*	0 263 13996 4
Priority Care *Mary Hawkins*	0 263 13997 2

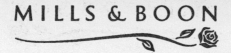

MILLS & BOON

NOVEMBER 1994 HARDBACK TITLES

Romance

Trial by Marriage *Lindsay Armstrong*	H4164	0 263 14133 0
Sweet Desire *Rosemary Badger*	H4165	0 263 14134 9
Angels Do Have Wings *Helen Brooks*	H4166	0 263 14135 7
Games Lovers Play *Rosemary Carter*	H4167	0 263 14136 5
Hot November *Ann Charlton*	H4168	0 263 14137 3
The Dating Game *Sandra Field*	H4169	0 263 14138 1
Reform of the Rake *Catherine George*	H4170	0 263 14139 X
No Ties *Rosemary Gibson*	H4171	0 263 14140 3
Moonshadow Man *Jessica Hart*	H4172	0 263 14141 1
Come Back Forever *Stephanie Howard*	H4173	0 263 14142 X
It Started with a Kiss *Mary Lyons*	H4174	0 263 14143 8
War of Love *Carole Mortimer*	H4175	0 263 14144 6
A Secret Infatuation *Betty Neels*	H4176	0 263 14145 4
A Physical Affair *Lynsey Stevens*	H4177	0 263 14146 2
Trial in the Sun *Kay Thorpe*	H4178	0 263 14147 0
A Burning Passion *Cathy Williams*	H4179	0 263 14148 9

LEGACY of LOVE

Crown Hostage *Joanna Makepeace*	M347	0 263 14163 2
The Reasons for Marriage *Stephanie Laurens*	M348	0 263 14164 0

LOVE ON CALL

Storm Haven *Marion Lennox*	D265	0 263 14241 8
In at the Deep End *Laura MacDonald*	D266	0 263 14242 6

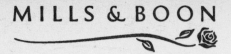

MILLS & BOON

NOVEMBER 1994 LARGE PRINT TITLES

Romance

The Fury of Love *Natalie Fox*	759	0 263 13935 2
The Last Illusion *Diana Hamilton*	760	0 263 13936 0
Dangerous Desire *Sarah Holland*	761	0 263 13937 9
Phantom Lover *Susan Napier*	762	0 263 13938 7
Wedding Bells for Beatrice *Betty Neels*	763	0 263 13939 5
Dark Victory *Elizabeth Oldfield*	764	0 263 13940 9
Love's Sting *Catherine Spencer*	765	0 263 13941 7
Edge of Danger *Patricia Wilson*	766	0 263 13942 5

LEGACY *of* LOVE

Serena *Sylvia Andrew*	0 263 14018 0
Hostage of Love *Valentina Luellen*	0 263 14019 9

LOVE ON CALL

Running Away *Lilian Darcy*	0 263 13998 0
The Senior Partner's Daughter *Elizabeth Harrison*	0 263 13999 9